eka

AN
ASHOKA CENTRE FOR
TRANSLATION
SERIES

ANITA AGNIHOTRI

SELECTED STORIES

TRANSLATED FROM
THE BENGALI
BY ARUNAVA SINHA

ekadā

First published in English as *Anita Agnihotri: Selected Stories* in 2026 by Ekadā, an imprint of Westland Books, a division of Nasadiya Technologies Private Limited, with the Ashoka Centre for Translation, Ashoka University

No. 269/2B, First Floor, 'Irai Arul', Vimalraj Street, Nethaji Nagar, Alapakkam Main Road, Maduravoyal, Chennai 600095

ISBN: 9788168873032

10 9 8 7 6 5 4 3 2 1

Typeset by Jojy Philip

Printed at Manipal Technologies Limited, Manipal

ANITA AGNIHOTRI

CONTENTS

INTRODUCTION

'Every art form is an expression of political consciousness'[1]

Anita Agnihotri began writing before she could write. As a small child, she composed poems in her head, reciting them aloud. Her mother transcribed them. Perhaps it was inevitable that, once she had started, she would never stop writing. Today, after seventy books, spanning novels, short story collections, poetry collections, essay compilations and children's writings, she's planning what might be her most expansive work: a novel situated in the time of the greatest upheavals in her home state of Bengal, from 1971 and earlier to 2021 and beyond.

Her fiction in general, and her short stories in particular, are urgent demonstrations of her ability to make literature from life. Few writers have lived and witnessed the extremes of existence in India as Agnihotri has. As an IAS officer who served for thirty-six years, from 1980 till her retirement in 2016, she was posted in towns and cities across the country, and in each case, she made it a point to go to the people whose welfare she was entrusted with to learn about the realities of their lives.

But it would be a mistake to assume that her fiction is a thinly veiled documentary based on what she has observed. 'To my mind, imagination is the primary component of literature,' Agnihotri said in an interview. To be sure, you cannot separate the harsh realities of the lives of her characters from universalities, but the things that happen to them, and the things they do, are unique to each individual in her stories. Avoiding the easy path of creating stock characters, she devotes her attention to thinking up flesh-and-blood women and men, and makes them confront the cataclysms that come their way. She builds character through the narrator's deeply involved observation—watching how people live and work, what their landscape looks like—and participation, which takes the form of exploring their hearts and minds as well as their doubts and despair and their joys and promises.

But this is not to say that it is always stories of humans versus circumstances that she writes. The relationships between people are of vital importance in her fiction. Her imagination weaves these relationships—and these stand challenged by the crises that loom large. It is through the particular that Agnihotri invites readers to create their own version of the larger truth that the stories point towards. 'When I write,' she has stated, 'there is a lot of detailing.'

For this, the writer uses her language. Critics often describe her use of the Bengali language as poetic or lyrical. Agnihotri has said that it is, in fact, the presence of nature in her writing that makes it seem this way. As a translator of her work, I find myself working primarily with her use of language. And it is in the way she paints with it that the entirety of her stories stands revealed. It should come as no surprise to know that Agnihotri does not plot her fiction intricately. She allows the flow of the characters to take over, but her beautiful prose—always customised to the specific demands of each story—creates the patterns which we as readers come to love.

Ironically, for someone who is punctilious about her use of the Bengali language, Agnihotri has spent most of her adult life outside the Bengali-speaking world. In the course of life and work, she has also acquired Hindi, Marathi and Odia, besides Bengali and English, of course. When posted in Odisha, she often sent her manuscripts to publishers from rural post offices in Koraput, Sambalpur, or Kalahandi. She has never occupied the drawing rooms of Kolkata's publishers and writers. And she has argued, Bengali is so alive as a language that 'without regular engagement with it, your writing can miss the mark'. Yet, she has pointed out that she would never have written many of the novels and short stories she is best known for had she stayed on in Kolkata teaching at a university, as her mother had wanted her to.

'Writing is my expression of freedom,' she once said in an interview. Freedom from the structured definition of her work in the Indian Administrative Service, of course, but also from the tyranny of singular models of development that frame the betterment of the country only as a particular form of economic growth. Reading Agnihotri's fiction makes it clear that she does not feign neutrality. She is palpably on the side of the poor and the oppressed—in every situation. 'Every art form is an expression of political consciousness,' she has said. 'From the subconscious, it flows into poetry, stories, novels.'

The stories in this collection are clear testimony to the themes around which Agnihotri weaves her short fiction. In stories like 'Sabotage', 'The Right to Information, or April 7' and 'The Deceivers', we see the grinding dehumanisation practised by the state over the decades. The marginalisation of workers and labourers, often leading to the erasure of identity, makes its presence felt in 'The Heat Chamber', 'In the Moonlight' and 'Sarojbala'. We see domestic tyranny and the battle for agency in action in stories like 'Submerged' and 'Rules of the Game', and even in 'The Last Samurai'. And themes of displacement and memory appear in stories such as 'Archaeomelancholy and the Water', 'The Poet's House' and 'Address of Oblivion'.

It isn't necessary to talk of Anita Agnihotri's stories. It is necessary to read them.

Arunava Sinha

SABOTAGE

When he returned home Shibaji went directly to the dining space. Turning the tap on at the sink, he washed his hands with liquid soap, rubbing them against each other repeatedly. His wife Smita had bought the pouch of soap a fortnight ago. Apparently this was the most hygienic way to wash one's hands. Smita had left today—the pouch was a little more than half full. He had developed this obsession with washing his hands about a year ago. Because it was a jarring sight, Smita would stop him sometimes with a movement of her eyes. Now that she wasn't here, Shibaji would wash his hands as often as he liked. Sub-Inspector Gaffoor Khan had died at this time last year. On the elderly side, he was a little plump, with a white moustache, not very fit physically. He had been promoted to sub-inspector after spending many years as a hawaldar in an area where there was no such thing as crime. Mile after mile of unpopulated land, dense jungles, interspersed by wide valleys full of shoots and leaves in a multitude of colours, and the celebrations of flowers. Intense poverty, a scarcity of schools and hospitals, and practically non-existent electricity. Even in the district headquarters, the power came and went at will, staying only a few hours each time. The Intelligence Bureau people sent secret reports from time to time in indecipherable scrawls—extremist organisations were spreading their roots in rural areas, conducting brainwashing sessions by night. They were handing out money to boys and girls, sporting equipment and books and leaflets too, and would soon start recruitment. All these notes remained in the in-trays on the desks in the police station. No one bothered to read them. At least, till Shibaji came, the practice of reading them did not exist. But even Shibaji had not been able to spare the time; he had been promoted only last year, and had joined as the superintendent of police for the district just about a week ago, which was when a landmine blew up a car belonging to the Tilda police station. Sub-Inspector Khan's and two constables' bodies. The constables' faces had been mutilated grotesquely, one of their bodies thrown into the bushes by a bungalow. There was no doubt that they were dead. When Shibaji reached the spot, the first thing he saw was Khan, sprawled beneath the sunlit sky, the yellow light mingling with his body, his arms spread out wide. He was the only declaration of peace amidst the monstrosity of the smashed jeep and the fragments of human bodies.

Assuming that Khan could still be sent to the hospital in the jeep accompanying his car, Shibaji had joined his driver and constables. Like unexpected, undeclared terror, blood poured out, reddening his hands. It had not been obvious that there was such a large, gaping wound precisely at the centre of Khan's back.

Afternoon had turned into evening before Shibaji had managed to sit down to a meal that day. Not much of a meal—a little vegetable soup and two chapatis. Smita had practically forced them on him. When he sat down to eat, Shibaji felt that his fingers still had bloodstains the colour of rust, and a raw smell. He had risen from the table to wash his hands with soap at the bathroom sink. And that was how he had acquired the habit. Every time there was news of death, injury or explosions, he had the urge to wash his hands. Was it obsessive-compulsive disorder? Shibaji had been working continuously for a year with the disorder; perhaps he would have to leave the world soon with his disorder intact.

He would have had to work as an additional SP for four years or so. The post of SP, though it meant moving some distance from the state capital, was a challenging one. Just as he was beginning to feel that there was no charm to being the second-in-command, he had been told of the promotion. Whereupon Shibaji had done something he didn't usually do, which was to return home at an unusual hour, put his arms around his sleeping wife and kiss her wildly. The posting order had only just been issued—this was a golden opportunity to take a week to join and use the time to meet both sets of parents in Delhi. The husband and wife were planning the trip at night, between lovemaking and sleep. In the morning came the summons from the Department of Home. Shibaji had been both surprised and pleased. He was welcomed effusively and offered tea in a virtually transparent cup and saucer of bone china. The home secretary was present, as was the inspector general of police. Astonished by the statement, 'So this is the courageous young man,' Shibaji heard the secretary say, 'He's even named after a fearless hero—Shibaji.'

Although he was thrown into doubt by the sudden discussion of courage and heroism, Shibaji was subsequently told that he would have to inform the ministry of the infrastructural problems faced by the police over there, and that the government was determined to provide the district with all its requirements.

Abandoning the lure of a week of what bureaucrats called 'joining leave', Smita, Tulika and he set off for the uncertain the very next day. Uncertain, because he had already gathered some feedback from his friends and senior officers. He had even got a sense of the fiery situation in the district. The Department of Home read reports that were even more flawless and timely than the ones which lazy police officers didn't bother to read in their village homes. Today Shibaji knew that he had been selected not because of his heroism but as a sacrificial goat.

The area was surrounded by hills, with a mountain stream flowing through it. A new district carved out of an old one. The Sadar office had been set up about ten years ago, but it was still not well-appointed. Travelling from the capital meant a fourteen-hour train journey, followed by a drive. Travelling by car took eighteen to twenty hours on bad roads. Winters were intensely cold, though the summers weren't unbearable. Although the timber mafia had cleared much of the jungle, the ancient forests had not yet been wiped out entirely. The rain wasn't insignificant, which was why trees kept growing unbidden all over the place—on the hillside, by the roads, on uncultivated land.

Tulika was only three. She used to go to a playschool when they lived in the city—not a significant form of education. She could be taught at home for now. Besides, there was always nature. The landscapes hereabouts were so delightful that an entire calendar could be made with them. After her wedding,

Smita had enrolled for a doctorate with Delhi University, but the work was proceeding at a slow pace, the fieldwork had not begun as yet. She wasn't particularly anxious at the outset of her journey into the uncertain with Shibaji—she was curious instead. The area wouldn't be a bad choice for her fieldwork. But as soon as they reached, the family as well as Shibaji's work environment had been enveloped in a sense of emptiness. No one moved to this place, no one wanted to. Even the district magistrate's post was vacant. How could this be possible? Several posts were vacant in different departments, including the revenue, rural development and police departments. Although allowances were higher here, no one wanted to be transferred to these parts. And those who did work here had been here for a long time, without being transferred. Because no one would accept transfers to this area. They had stagnated in the same posts in the same district for thousands of years, incapable of—and even opposed to—change.

Shibaji worked very hard. Attempts to improve the skills of his team, visiting the farms and the villages, establishing contact with people, arranging for fresh weapons and ammunition, and yet he experienced an infinite sense of exhaustion every evening. As though he had been knocked out of his orbit and was falling headlong into a deep black emptiness. After Khan's death, Shibaji had asked for four platoons of armed constables for surveillance and patrolling. Having knocked repeatedly on closed doors, he had finally been given three companies of forces—three months later. They were completely unfamiliar with the forests, the foothills, and the towns and villages hereabouts. After several months of purposeless movement and sleep, along with bouts of malaria, they had gone back in disarray. Shibaji had realised that there was no point learning the techniques of unarmed combat, but what was he to do anyway? He was now in the same situation as the rest of the people stagnating in the district without a future. He doubted whether there would ever be a replacement for him. Shibaji had been earmarked for valour and sacrifice.

The warmth of September gave way to autumn in the forest areas. Fresh flowers sprung up on the sandbanks in the river, and the jungle of the night began to smile with a profusion of yellow sage flowers. A deep crimson moon rose at the onset of evening, its reddish hue turning gradually to fiery orange and then silver. Sitting alone in the veranda, sometimes with her daughter in her lap, Smita watched all of this, but none of it made a mark on her. She was like a mirror, whose body existed only to reflect things, without a heart. When would Shibaji return, she wondered in her chair in the veranda. Was he in his office or had he gone off to some village or town somewhere? She had told him over and over again that, wherever he might go, he should return before sunset. 'As if it's safe even by daylight,' Shibaji had responded with a ruthless smile. What else could Smita have done but tremble at this? There was no opportunity to send her daughter to school, and even if there had been, she would probably not have done it. But it wasn't as though she was home-schooling Tulika. The picture books and toys were locked away in cupboards. So were boxes of beautiful saris and salwar-kameez, along with the yellow, pink and white baby frocks for her daughter. Where would they wear all this to? All they had here was anxiety and terror—there was no happiness in her heart. Smita didn't let the tablecloth hang low over the sides of the dining table.

Who knew whether something deadly was hidden beneath or not? Before going to bed at night she combed the corners of the room, the space beneath the bed, the folds of the curtains. Everyone at home was on the verge of suffering from obsessive-compulsive disorder. The building was originally the sub-divisional inspection bungalow. It wasn't exactly a house, for there was a claustrophobic air everywhere, except in the veranda at the back. Heavy curtains, small windows, the sitting room directly in front of the veranda, and a room on either side of it. This building had been chosen as the SP's residence after the new district was formed. Two or three Adivasi locals worked in the kitchen and cleaned the house. They had even brought an aged woman from Shibaji's office to look after Tulika. But Smita didn't approve of any of them. She didn't even allow the old woman anywhere near her daughter. And sometimes she felt apprehensive too. What if this distrust on her part provoked anger or revolt? This fear made Smita change her strategy at times. She laughed and joked with them, exchanging meaningless conversations. But through it all she remained cautious, just in case they made any indiscreet confessions.

Despite being neck-deep in uncertainty, they did manage to chat and smile through dinner—Shibaji and Smita. Tulika joined them if she was awake, perched not on a chair but on the table, pushing the pots and bowls away with her arms. Shibaji laughed away Smita's shift of strategy. 'What rubbish—all this is speculation! These are all ordinary, poor people, forced to work here for a living. They're under pressure from both sides—the police on one side and extremists on the other. All they want is to remain silent. They cannot be made to talk. I have learnt all this from my trips to the villages for first-hand information.'

At night they slept snuggling up to one another; Smita wasn't even willing to let her daughter sleep on a bed of her own. She had dreamt of a renewed, deeper intimacy when they moved to this desolate area. But now even the desire for a relationship had vanished—they clung to each other out of fear. The grassy fields with trees that lay beyond the veranda at the back looked magical in the moonlight. The forest and the earth were exactly as Smita had expected them to be; only, their unquenchable thirst had dried up everything else.

Peace reigned for about four months following Khan's killing, as though nothing had ever happened. In the middle of winter, a remote police outpost was attacked. Only a single guard with a stick was on duty, the rest being out on patrol. His blood-smeared, bullet-ridden body lay there till the next morning. There was neither mobile phone coverage nor a phone at the outpost. Information took a long time to travel. Who were the attackers? Probably not a large group of people. There was no torching or looting. The killing was a signature of sorts. The attackers had left after signing.

What is it you want? Even if not with these precise words, this was what Shibaji tried to find out during his attempts to make contact with people. His eyes asked the same question of newlyweds in shell jewellery, of men afflicted by old age, of pregnant women. I know what would help, but the key to these solutions is not in my hands. Your right to enter the forests has been curtailed, your tube wells don't work, your schools have leaking roofs, your hospitals have no doctors or nurses, your women die during childbirth, your children are born in darkness, your sick die in the darkness. Yes, I know all this, but why don't you speak up? Are all of you mute? Who are the people you have summoned to settle things with us—they know of nothing but weapons. So many constables and so many middle-level inspectors have died. Does anyone know whose fault it is that they were killed? Who is going to hunt the killers down? The forests are dense, the paths are hidden, the villages nestle in the folds of the mountains, we don't have enough people to track the killers. How will we know who the murderers are? What's the use of searching, when almost anyone might be the killer?

Shibaji muttered to himself at home these days. So Smita had to keep an eye on him too. His mumbles and frequent washing of hands gave birth to a vague fear in her mind. Would they have to live here in exile till death?

Barely a year had passed, but they felt as though they were living inside a closed box. Shibaji was trying his utmost to get out, of course, travelling the long distance to the capital with his entreaty. It wasn't possible to meet the minister on one's own initiative, without being summoned. The home secretary had been too busy to meet him. He had got two and a half minutes with the director general of police, who had informed him that a transfer order was impossible in less than three years. But yes, the armoury would be refurbished to strengthen his hand. The armoury? Low walls, half the ceiling comprising sheets of corrugated tin, a damp, ancient building. They had submitted a plan for a new structure, and nine or ten months had passed since then. But then that involved expenses; the arms and ammunition would arrive first, since they had been ordered earlier.

The store of modern weapons which he had built carefully was looted. They had come. In flocks, one might say. Twenty-five or thirty outsiders in a tiny, sleepy district town. You could definitely say they had flocked in. They ate at roadside restaurants, smoked in front of the cinema hall. Split into small groups, they included girls too. The local people didn't understand their language, which was a mixture of the border tongue and Hindi. All this came to light afterwards, however.

All but one of the nine or ten guards at the armoury were killed in the unexpected attack, a celebration of fire and blood. Although out of practice for years, the guards had been the first to open fire but hadn't been able to save themselves. The militants had left after piling the weapons in a small truck. Shibaji was at the other end of the district that day, in an area surrounded by dense forests. It took two and a half hours just to get back. The entire operation was completed in thirty-five minutes. Shibaji went to the spot, without having had the chance to wash his hands. Bindu Parja was present. The only female guard to have survived, she had watched the rest of them die. She had stood till the end with her gun, emptied of cartridges. Her eighteen-year-old son had burnt to cinders in front of her eyes—he had recently joined as a temporary sentry. The bomb had set his body on fire.

When she saw Shibaji, Bindu forgot formal protocol. Instead of a salute, her heartrending cries rose in the air—it wasn't so much crying as it was the screams of a speared animal. Laying a cold, stiff hand on Shibaji's chest that night, Smita told him repeatedly, 'Quit this job, there's no need. Quit, you're an engineer after all, you can get a private-sector job, we can manage without a job for some time …'

Decisions like these weren't easy to take. The enquiry into the raid, arranging compensation for the dead and paying for the treatment of the wounded took a month and a half. The national media had flashed the news for several successive days. Smita's parents had called them tearfully. The same request—come away at once, all of you, if you can't quit, take leave.

Leave. The most priceless commodity at the moment. The application for leave was rejected at once. Those who could not approve anything on time could reject things with flawless alacrity. Take leave now? Aren't you aware of the fact that the Union home minister is coming for a review, with a dozen central officers? You'd better get the helipad ready instead, several helicopters will be coming.

Eventually it was decided that Smita would go to Delhi with Tulika. And Shibaji would try for leave again after the minister's tour had ended. Or else …

'I'll quit. I promise, Smita. I can't take this tension, this pressure, day after day anymore. Already my blood pressure is fluctuating, I've developed cholesterol too. What's the point of wasting life this way, you're right, Smita …'

Weeping late into the night, without sleeping, Smita had left in great anguish. Shibaji had seen her off on the train from the major junction in the adjoining district. Tuli was hurt too, hiding her face in her mother's breast and refusing to speak. She kept displaying a moist little finger to indicate that she had quarrelled with him. The junction was two hours away. He had already received a couple of text messages from Smita on the way back—are you okay? Take care. As though something would happen any moment.

Back home, Shibaji went directly to the dining space and washed his hands thoroughly, using the hygienic liquid soap that Smita had bought.

The food was not laid out on the dining table as it was every day. The napkins, knives, forks, plates—everything was missing. Shibaji peeped into the kitchen—no one there. The breakfast cornflakes and the milk were scattered all over. Sukhan, Ram and Pandavi were nowhere to be seen. The entire house was empty. Strange! Their presence was so natural that Shibaji did not register their absence at first. He went out into the garden at the back through the kitchen door. It wasn't exactly a garden—a small patch of grass, and then a host of wild plants and vines. The forest seemed to have paused deferentially, waiting for an invitation to enter the house.

It was a desolate afternoon. Wild ducks and skylarks kept calling in a deserted emptiness. A yellow leaf or two drifted to the ground in the melancholy sunlight. As soon as Shibaji stepped out, the forest charged at him. On heavy but silent footsteps. The curtain of green coalesced into the shape of a barrel. Dry gunpowder had been stuffed into it centuries ago.

Shibaji's mobile phone lay on the dining table. By now innumerable messages had gathered in it—of love, of tears, of anxiety, of rage. Now the calls kept coming ... the ringtone echoed through the empty house.

Shibaji's fingers were still smelling of liquid soap.

THE HEAT CHAMBER

'Poobi! E…i Poobi!' Sheetli called her from the back, giggling.

Poobi ran off, remnants of food still on her fingers.

She was dressed in a floppy, faded gown, the one she was eating in. Hardly an elaborate meal—merely two ladles of rice scraped off the bottom of the pot. Poobi was waiting with a few stray shrimps and a sea of curry on her plate, confident that her mother would give her all the rice. She was chewing the shrimp shells with great concentration. But Poobi's mother Chinta gave Sheetli the entire portion of rice without a second thought; Sheetli's plate was dry, without any curry on it. And didn't their mother know how big Poobi's appetite was? She was absolutely famished this morning. The lamp at home had been put out after they had eaten the rice cooked last evening, as it always was—after which had passed an entire night, the dawn, and the early morning, with the sun a little stronger now. They would eat the rice preserved overnight by soaking it in water, with a little salt and lime added for taste, before going off to work. She could have accepted the extra rice being given to Sheetli, despite the raging hunger in her belly. But why did Chinta have to say, 'This girl's stomach is like a bottomless pit, never full,' at which Sheetli began to lick her fingers and laugh, rocking from side to side. Poobi couldn't take it anymore—tossing her plate aside, she ran out the door with the food particles still on her fingers.

An angry cuckoo kept calling from the sunburnt greenery of the neem tree. After a long spell of calling 'ku-hu, ku-hu …', it changed its tune abruptly to call 'drishti dyan, drishti dyan'. On other days the two sisters laughed about the cuckoo's anger, but Poobi couldn't care less today. Shame and misery steamed out of her ears. She walked, towards the river along the trail between the acacias and the bamboo groves, nudging the tamarind, guava and mango trees.

The river was very close to their house. But it wasn't visible because the path leading to it was uneven. The river preferred to remain below the line of sight.

Its sandy yellow beach was long, its bluish currents forming three or four separate streams. The trees across the river were visible from the house where Poobi and her family lived, while the bushes and woods on this bank concealed the enormous expanse of water, but still the scent of the river wafted up. The river had a smell of its own, of flowing water, of the scraps floating along with it—leaves and vines, dead chicks, lumps of sand loosened from the river bank—the combined smell of all of these; and the sky above the river had a different sort of colour too. On many afternoons, if she had a full stomach and a holiday from work, Poobi sat on the stoop at the front door, gazing at the river. Today, however, she had no time for all this. Passing swiftly along the path which ran uphill and downhill alternately, disregarding the thorns and pebbles poking her feet, Poobi plunged into the river. Not to die, though. Both the sisters could swim so well that they would need a silted well and not a river to drown.

Floating on the water, and taking a couple of dips, Poobi allowed her tears to flow into the river. Why did she have so many tears inside? When Poobi grew up and had her own family, her own house and children, she would make rice in a huge brass pot, the kind that the Dases had in their kitchen. She would season the matar daal with ghee, and yes … big lobsters, fried prime cuts of hilsa … even if she had ten children, none of them would run short of food. Lots of red, small-grained rice—she wouldn't cook like a miser the way her mother did, skimping on things, she would cook properly …

Schools of tiny fish swam along the strong current—if she had a gamchha she could have caught some of them. Poobi's rage had finally ebbed away, leaving her calm. She neither had a gamchha with her now, nor a change of clothes; she would have to run sopping wet along the fiery hot path. Ishh! As she swam, submerged up to her neck in the water, Poobi saw that the girls from Meherpara were here to bathe, one or two of them with buckets to take some water back after their baths. In the monsoon, the water turned turbid. People didn't drink the river water in those months. They had as many as three tube wells in the area, but the older people still preferred the water from the river.

'Ei Poobi!'

Sheetli was standing on the bank with her gamchha. She wasn't laughing anymore. Maybe their mother had told her not to. Poobi didn't look at her, deliberately. Muffling her giggles, Sheetli said, 'Not going to work today? Ma was asking.'

She was late. Had Poobi been creating excuses, unknown to herself, for not going to work today? Remnants of the tears that had collected in her heart had risen to gather at her throat now, even after most of them had flowed away with the river. The Dases' clerk had sent for muri and fried dumplings last evening—his name was Basanta. How had he got to know that Poobi was always ravenous? She had never had a meal in his presence, after all. They were never given anything to eat at their workplace. Poobi had long been used to suppressing her hunger. When she came home she gulped down her meal. There were days when she couldn't even wait long enough to check whether her mother and sister had eaten.

Yesterday Basanta had given Poobi twice as much of the muri and dumplings as the others. Poobi was eating with great concentration—so much concentration that she had got the oil from the dumplings on her nose—when she suddenly realised that Basanta's hand on her back was wandering. It wasn't so much a hand as a paw, on the nape of her neck, then lower down to her waist. Basanta stood behind a pillar, shielding her from view while he talked and laughed with someone else, his hand roaming about on Poobi's back. She suddenly felt as though she were a beast—a sheep or a goat, or perhaps a pig, but not a human. Human beings had two arms and two legs, but in her case all four limbs were legs … why did she feel this way? Poobi twisted herself into a standing position, she was done eating by then, it was time to rinse her hands. But her sobs had gathered in her throat, refusing to subside. She couldn't gulp them down with a drink of water. Even with her limited intelligence Poobi could make out that there was a connection between her appetite and Basanta's paws.

Which was why shame, humiliation, fear and rage had all balled up in her heart. As soon as the wick was lit with two ladles of rice, her heart burst into flames.

Her wet clothes sticking to her back, the fabric tripping her, the gamchha wrapped around her body, Poobi decided as she walked that she would go to work. Forty rupees at the end of the day. And the work was seasonal. She couldn't spurn the money. What would Basanta do? He was paid a salary by the Dases. Perhaps he earned a little more than Poobi.

The neighbourhood that Poobi's family lived in was in a corner of the village, by the path that led out of the village towards the field near Domohona. Haarimuchis lived there, in small houses with low ceilings. The roads weren't clean. Not many Brahmins or Kayasths lived in this village. It was dominated by Mehers. There were looms in every home, clacking all day, with the sounds of moving shuttles. A dense forest crouched at the feet of the hills that rose like a wall of clouds to the north of the village. Although timber-thieves had cut down many of the trees, there was still a profusion of sal, teak, myrobalan, neem and bamboo. There were ancient seats of arjun and bridelia trees too, where Santhal and Munda tribals cultivated silkworms and braved the sun, storms and rain under an open sky.

Poobi and the other workers spun silk thread with foot-operated machines. At one end of the village was the large building of the cooperative. About two dozen machines had been set up on the first floor. Another group of women worked on the veranda outside. Their work involved softening the silkworms in soapy water. Hooking the tiny head of thread peeping out of the body of the silkworm like golden down, the machine kept unravelling it, continuously. And a thread of silk like a strand of golden hair, even lighter than hair, was wound around the bobbin.

From ten in the morning to five in the evening. Wages in proportion to the quantity of thread spun. Between thirty-five and forty rupees. That too seasonal—the season in which silkworms were brought. Once upon a time, twenty or thirty years ago, a mountain of silkworms would gather in the veranda downstairs. Everything had turned upside down since the gale of seven years ago. The coconuts turned out hollow; the trees stopped growing, looking emaciated; the heat increased; either it rained continuously without respite or the clouds blew away to a foreign land, leaving no trace of rain. Silk cultivation could not thrive in such uncertain conditions. The caterpillars died prematurely while feasting on leaves, and the production of silkworms dropped. With large numbers of people across the country spinning silk and weaving it on looms, the cooperative from Poobi's village also had to queue up in the city to buy silkworms. But the situation had begun to improve once Das-babu became the president of the cooperative. For he had both a personal quota and one on behalf of the cooperative. 'With so many people dependent on me for their livelihoods, I'm not ashamed to tell a lie now and then.' Siddha-pishi from Meherpara would say bitingly at once, 'Why should anyone starve … there's no reason for anyone to starve … if the women from even the Buno and Bagdi and Chamar families start spinning silk …'

A few years ago, Poobi would laugh along with the rest at this. She didn't laugh anymore. She knew the finger was pointing at her. Her dark cheeks reddened in humiliation.

Before leaving home, Poobi glanced at her own reflection in the mirror hanging from a peg on the wall. Was she really very dark? Even when she ran an oil-smeared hand through her hair, its reddish hue didn't go. Still, she combed her hair and drew a light layer of body powder across her face. She had a total of two dresses to wear outside the house. Two sets of salwar-kameez, neither with matching colours for the top and bottom halves. Both the salwars were torn near the ankles, hanging together thanks to repeated darning. Despite her huge appetite and all the abuse that her mother heaped on her for it, Poobi had no fat on her. Her collarbones jutted out, her breasts had not filled out, her bottom was not fleshy even at eighteen. None of this had occurred to her earlier, but she was aware of all this now that Basanta had run his hand across her back. She had had to stop going to school in order to spin thread. When there was no work once the season had ended, she picked up Sheetli's book, her heart breaking. There was no telling how much longer Sheetli would go to school either. But Poobi would try to ensure she went as long as possible. Their father hadn't been home in a long time now. No one knew whether he was even alive. Their mother's expression was always dark and rigid these days, not changing even when their father came up in the course of conversation.

There was work at brick kilns across the state border. The contractors came, offering advance payments and taking away between five hundred and a thousand people at a time, piling them into trucks. People were packed like sardines into rows of living quarters resembling tents. Many of them even took their wives and children—who would cook for them during the six months they would spend there? But their father hadn't wanted to take them along. Apparently life was very hard there.

They made people work from dawn till midnight, the children pulling out the bricks from the moulds with their tender fingers, while the women made the moulds and the men fired the bricks in the kiln. Their hands and faces were blackened by the heat from the fire and the high temperatures. Yet the workers and their children were beaten up if they made the smallest of mistakes. The wives were molested at night. They lived like cattle, without the slightest privacy of a home of their own. NGO activists had often brought back corpses with blisters on their shoulders and backs and their limbs fractured. These things never changed. Their father had not wanted Poobi and Sheetli and their mother to have this kind of existence. Which was why he stayed on over there. He had not been home in over two years. The money arrived at the post office once every six months. Their mother went to collect it. This money was the thread linking the three of them to the girls' father. Every six months, Poobi's heart was in a turmoil of misery. What if the postmaster said the money had not arrived? Check later. If the money really did not arrive, would that mean their father was dead?

Their mother said it made no difference, for they were all dead already. Poobi knew she said this because she was hurt. When Chinta was exhausted with all the work she had to do every day—doing the dishes, cleaning the home, spinning thread, gathering wood, drawing water—she wondered what good it was having a man in her life if she couldn't have even a bit of comfort. But Poobi was sure that she was alive—that all three of them were alive. Although it was only one day at a time. There was nothing after the lantern was put out every evening. But still. When Poobi awoke in the wee hours of the morning out of sheer hunger, when there was still a purple-pink darkness outside, when the cuckoo had just started calling, and when the dawn breeze was making the coral tree near the fence sway a little ... Poobi was flooded with a wonderful joy. Another day had broken on earth. All around Poobi. Letting herself float on the river, she felt that this water, the sparkling sand, the pouting little fish, all of it had been laid out by someone just for her. She was in a pleasant frame of mind when she went to the factory after combing her hair, powdering herself and slipping on her sandals. Two hundred or even two hundred and fifty rupees at the end of the week. Although her mother took it all, five or ten rupees did make their way back to Poobi, to buy trinkets or some food. Maybe there was something else beyond all this—a steep downhill slope, or a dry riverbed, or a long, black wall without a window. But Poobi didn't dwell on those. She waved the worry away with both her arms. What if her father didn't return, what if she was suddenly asked to leave the factory, what if Sheetli got married, her mother died, and the house began to crumble like an anthill—what would Poobi do then? It was far better to live one day at a time.

Poobi went to the factory, hoping that Basanta wouldn't be there. Not that it was much of a factory—just a sprawling building of the cooperative's, standing amidst a jungle of weeds and bushes. About two dozen looms on the ground floor, clacking away all day—the shuttle moving in and out like a rudderless dinghy, silkworms being boiled in warm water set on rows of clay ovens in the first-floor veranda before being washed with soapy water. The foot-operated machines used by

Poobi and the others standing inside the room. If Poobi and the rest were workers, this was certainly a factory. The cooperative was supposed to be for members, but as everyone knew, it was only nominally a cooperative. The Dases had actually turned it into a factory of their own. Rajeeb Das was the president of the cooperative. As far as he was concerned, members, workers and daily labourers were all one and the same. He owned over a thousand looms spread across twenty or so villages in the area. All of them got their thread and colours from Das-babu's warehouse and received wages for weaving fabric with these. They were called weavers formally, but in fact they were loom labourers.

A labourer was a labourer. Whether you're spinning silk or weaving the yarn into fabric. Das-babu bought silkworms from the tribals and got Poobi and the others to spin thread out of them. So they were labourers of thread-spinning—a group of men and a bunch of women then wove this thread at the looms.

But how strange—the factory was almost empty today. Basanta wasn't there. Ten people were sitting at the looms downstairs. When they saw Poobi, they said, you're very late. Everyone had vanished. Poobi stomped up the stairs, and then came back. There really wasn't anyone. The place was deserted. The machines were silent. Everything was still.

Das-babu had gone off to the riverside with the supervisor and manager. There was no one to look after things. No work. No money, either. Poobi felt a rage building. Forty rupees. They would get it only if the owner willed it—not otherwise.

Thick clouds gathered in the sky on these May afternoons. From time to time nor'westers appeared, raising a storm and breaking off branches and leaves from trees. On other days there was no rain or squall, only dense clouds that blew away on the wind. The clouds had gathered today too, the air and the earth were hot, but still the clouds raised hopes of rain. Buying herself two rupees' worth of muri and peanuts, Poobi strolled to the river. Five or six of the girls who had turned up at the factory were loitering, but Poobi had been in a foul mood since yesterday. Siddha-pishi and Basanta had rolled up inside her head like a two-headed monster, which was why she didn't feel like talking to anyone.

There used to be an abandoned room on the land that Das-babu owned personally. Salt-dampened walls, broken tiles on the roof. It had been demolished, and fresh foundations had been laid, the walls had come up, the roof would be laid soon. Splinters of wood, sections of bricks and red pebbles lay scattered around the building, while a brown coucal hopped around inside the empty structure. No one she knew was there. The Munda was an aged farmer, resting his chin on the head of his stick and grinning at her. A shaggy mop of white hair, bare-bodied. Dressed in his tribal clothes, he had grime in his toenails. Poobi had seen such people in the arjun forest in Suanpur—her father had taken her. For twenty, thirty, forty years or even longer, these people had been cultivating silkworms in the jungle. Neither the sun nor storms and rain could deter them—everything blew over their heads.

'What's going on here, Dadu?'

'Ushmakothi. Heat chamber,' answered the old man at once.

Silence.

Poobi's heart beat faster.

She was used to seeing the silkworms being boiled in pots every day, but now the owner had made arrangements for carnage in the heat chamber. Actually, a virtual mountain of silkworms had gathered from the last season and this one. Boiling them in the pots could no longer produce enough yarn—they needed more. The silk looms were not being fed thread to weave. Aluminium pipes would now be fixed on the walls. Smoke from a fire would be piped through them, generating searing heat in the entire room. As hot as an actual fire, it wouldn't let people enter the room. Thousands of chrysalises would be lying on trays, the plump black moths sleeping inside with their wings folded, waiting to see the light of the world. They would never break through the hard walls of the chrysalises to emerge outside. Das-babu wouldn't let them. Once the moth had escaped the shell, its thread was of no use. The fine silk thread could not be spun. Imprisoned in that room for four or five hours, they would boil to death. Thousands of worms, millions of worms. Only then would Poobi and the rest of them earn their wages for spinning thread, only then would the looms of the weavers operate. How much could the boiling water in the pots handle, after all? The heat chamber would bring death to hundreds of kilos of moths—every day. Poobi shivered.

Stupid moths! What kind of life was this! Did they also dream of the night passing and a new day on its way—like Poobi's parents and Sheetli did every day—and mistake this for life! And then they left the world without the chance of unfurling their wings even once.

The old man was following Poobi, tapping on the ground with his stick. A smile suffused his toothless face. He had a stubble on his cheeks. It had rained somewhere in the distance—its smell was flowing in on a cool wind.

Grasshoppers flew about beneath the clouds. The oleander and magnolia trees by the river shook in the strong gusts of wind.

'What time is it, khuki? What time?'

Tossing a peanut into her mouth, Poobi said, 'I don't have a watch.'

'Don't have a watch,' the old man repeated to himself.

'It's going to rain. Where will you go?'

The old man didn't answer. Poobi knew he belonged to one of the villages inside the jungle at the base of the hill—Suanpur, Bibhangatali, or Amdari. A silk cultivator had suddenly wandered into the weavers' village, a cultivator who nurtured silkworms with the warmth and affection of his own heart.

Poobi had once spent an entire day in Suanpur with her father in torrential rain. She had been quite young then—ten or eleven. She used to go to school. Inside the dense arjun forest she had seen the freshly hatched, plump, tender caterpillars gorging on piles of leaves and growing. Rain or shine, these bare-bodied people with sticks in their hands ran about all day trying to protect and nurture the worms so that they might grow, chasing crows away loudly, smearing the tips of their sticks with homemade glue to trap hornets. When they had eaten their fill, the fleshy worms ejected thread from their mouths, using it to fasten themselves to stalks of leaves, and then spun a hard brown shell around themselves. Eventually hundreds of brown, wild chrysalises were found suspended from every tree in the jungle—and the Munda and Juang Santhals were still chasing away the crows, rats and hornets, and protecting the branches from the rain with their umbrellas …

Had her father also wanted to protect Poobi—Poobi, her mother, Sheetli, all of them—the same way? But would Poobi survive? The Dases' heat chamber would draw the smoke from the fire into the room and murder all of them.

Poobi and the others worked with death. Each of the worms left hundreds of threads behind. That was what Poobi and the rest spun, making yarn for the weavers to use on their looms.

What use was it to shiver now after dealing in death?

'Poobi, ei Poobi, listen …'

Looking over her shoulder, she found Basanta calling out to her. He had a pile of bricks on a van-rickshaw, for use at the building.

Turning to him with a grin, the old man asked, 'What time is it, khoka?'

When Poobi looked at Basanta, her rage from yesterday didn't return. She felt a stab of compassion, in fact. A sharp compassion. Look at the fool, bearing bricks for the carnage. He cannot sense the heat from the fire.

Her hunger slithered awake near her navel … roaring … it would bite any moment now …

SUBMERGED

'Where do you think you're going? There's no need.'

Still the woman went to the kitchen, smiling gently. She was about five feet five, looking more incisive in her blue salwar-kameez. You would have to take your eyes away from her face to find out just how far below her waist her long plait ended. So for now, Soumya told himself that the way she had parted her hair on the right and allowed her locks to fall over her forehead was a little odd, like a brow that had never been married …

'I'm warming some rice for you. You're a Bangali-babu, after all, how can you do without rice …'

I've been doing without many other things, Soumya thought to himself. Not even the remotest chance of getting any fish here …

He did get warm rice on his plate, though, long white grains of it. Anyone who now expected moong daal with this had to be an idiot. Pouring an unfamiliar light brown liquid into a steel bowl, Amrita said, 'I made pithla for you.'

Stirring this deep anguish of besan, Soumya said with a sigh, 'May I have a green chilli?'

'Of course.'

Bringing him a green chilli and a thin slice of lemon in a small bowl, Amrita said, making an O with her mouth, 'Babu-moshoy!'

His desperation for rice—and with it, his concentration on his plate—had abated. Melancholy was writ large on her forehead. Were the corners of her eyes a shade red, or had those eyes actually filled with tears? Soumya lacked the finesse to discern such things by neon light.

He was here from Calcutta for about a week, despatched by his newspaper. Satyesh Bagchi had provided him with the contact number, address and everything else. The satyagraha over water in the flooded valley would begin around the middle of the monsoon. The details of the preparations. The numerous changes of course during twenty-five years of the movement. Many social organisations had become part of the protests. Discussions with their members. The leader was nowhere to be seen. She was on her way—that was the rumour every day. The phone in Sanjay Deshmukh's office wouldn't stop ringing. Soumya would have to take the train back on Saturday whether she had arrived or not. 'Don't worry, young man,' Sanjay Deshmukh said, clapping him on the back, 'since you've come all this way, you won't have to go back disappointed. I will make sure you meet her.'

'Don't worry, bhai sahib,' Amrita had said, her eyes on the floor. 'If he has promised, it will happen. No one can turn him down.'

Amrita had appeared to be the classic Indian wife devoted to her husband. But she was a completely modern woman when it came to her speech and behaviour—her English was riddled with errors in verbs. The office, admissions and the hostel at

Sanjay Deshmukh's school were virtually under her control. Which was why Soumya didn't mind when she repeated the same question smilingly.

'Please tell me what Meena-tai said about me.'

'Nothing much, honestly. She just said that Amrita's very nice, as capable of looking after the home as she is of doing things outside of it.'

'Tchah, you're not telling me, because you won't tell me directly …' Amrita took the dishes away and mopped the floor swiftly with a wet rag. Soumya heard her putting the dishes away in the kitchen.

He was standing by the draw-well now with a pot of water to rinse his hands. Paved with cement, the area was in the shade thanks to several tall plants. Night jasmine and pinwheel. Mossy leaves and dust particles of different hues floated on the water. Hesitant to rinse his mouth with this water, Soumya used the contents of the pot to wash his hands and mouth cursorily.

A strong wind had sprung up. Perhaps it would rain again at night. The rain was welcome. It was scorching hot in this hilly area. The saving grace was the monsoon clouds that had been gathering for a few days. Otherwise, Soumya would have been worried about falling ill because of the sun. It was hot and humid in Calcutta, of course, but the temperature hadn't crossed thirty-seven degrees. And besides, it was a matter of what you were used to.

Since Sanjay Deshmukh wouldn't be home all day, Soumya had chosen to visit his house in the evening. What else was there for him to do in this tiny, unfamiliar town, where only the Satpura hills and their cousins stretched across the horizon? Since he had Vilasrao Bhonsle's address in his diary, he had spent some time there. Vilasrao was a veteran worker of the Sarvodaya movement. An Ayurvedic doctor with a flowing grey beard, he was a short and squat elderly man dressed in a khadi shirt and pyjamas. Bringing Soumya some tea and chanachur, Vilasrao's daughter-in-law Meena had wanted to know where he would be staying. A lively middle-aged woman, already greying slightly at the temples, with a pearl nose stud.

Yes, Meena Bhonsle had indeed sung Amrita's praises, just as Soumya had told her.

When her father-in-law went into his room to fetch the newspaper files, Meena had asked, her eyes dancing, 'How is Amrita? Did you know she isn't a local?'

Meanwhile Vilasrao entered, clearing his throat, and proceeded to explain the history of the freedom movement in the district to Soumya. Amrita was abandoned. As his daughter-in-law knew, the veteran Sarvodaya leader always cleared his throat, wagging his beard, when he sensed scandals being discussed.

Amrita brought small pieces of cardamom on a crystal plate, along with thinly sliced areca nuts. 'When will you eat?' asked Soumya, helping himself to a piece of cardamom with his fingertips.

'A late meal tonight.' Amrita dimpled. 'My husband won't be back till midnight. I don't know whether he's eating at home.'

'Do you wait up for him every night?'

'How could I not?' answered Amrita, drawing an embroidered sheet over her sleeping son. 'All I can do now is wait.'

The school stood in the middle of an enormous field. The hills flowed all around in pleasantly twisting lines. The rectangular building was single-storeyed, with a veranda running down its length. The classrooms, laboratory, computer hall and office room were all located in this building.

On the other side of the undulating surface of the field stood the as-yet-incomplete hostel, a three-storeyed building. Not all the windows had acquired shutters yet. Behind it was a makeshift bathroom with a tin roof. And finally, the Deshmukhs' house, with three or four other small houses in between. Signboards of tin attached to their walls said, 'Gurukul'. That is to say, had the previous headmaster and maths teacher not left out of frustration at a succession of vegetarian meals, their clothes would have been seen hanging on lines in front of these houses.

Soumya had been accommodated in one of these. But the town was so far away that he was forced to eat both breakfast and dinner at the Deshmukhs'. Otherwise, all his money would have been spent on autorickshaw fare.

It was ten at night now. Soumya should be on his way. He could go back to his room and try to read or write. The rooms were infested with insects of different shapes and sizes, all emitting bizarre sounds. Had the rooms turned into their seasonal dens because they had remained under lock and key a long time? He had to wrap a light sheet around his ears when he slept. This was on Amrita's suggestion. Large ants could crawl into the ears and bite—and that could be dangerous.

Sitting cross-legged on the bed, Amrita closed her oval eyes for a moment. Her nose stud did not glint this time. Looking directly at Soumya, she said, 'Did you know that I'm not a Hindu?'

Soumya was a little surprised, a trifle annoyed too. Was she expecting him to recoil in shock? What did a person's religion matter? People here were still living in the nineteenth century. But, summoning a smile to his lips, he said, 'Really? It never occurred to me.'

'Meena-tai really didn't say anything to you?'

'Believe me, she didn't. But why all these thoughts after all this time, Amrita?'

'Because my time is running out.'

Soumya shuddered. An image of a horrifying outcome of some sort dangled its legs over his heart. A dusty, arid desert stretching into the distance seemed to be visible through the cracks in Deshmukh's family—and yet there was such a show of activities, people, phone calls, a busy life …

'Don't you know what happened this morning? Didn't you hear anything afterwards?'

A baffled Soumya shook his head. Was any family free of such conflicts? But he did feel unhappy at the thought that someone as well-known and important as Sanjay Deshmukh could flare up over such an insignificant incident. He edited one newspaper and owned another. Everyone in the district knew who he was. A powerful and influential man.

Soumya's fault was that he had blurted out the truth. He could have kept it to himself instead.

'I hope you've got tea and breakfast,' Sanjay had asked him by the draw-well with a smile. Soumya hadn't bathed yet, but he was famished, unable to overcome his languor without a cup of tea.

'Not yet,' Soumya had answered casually, shaking his head. Was a complaint concealed in the 'yet'?

Sanjay had walked back into the house with angry steps and said something, the answer to which, naturally, had not been audible to Soumya where he was. But a fear had leapt into his heart without warning. Because he had unwillingly happened to catch sight of Sanjay beating up the servant at the hostel mercilessly earlier that morning. It hadn't even been properly light yet—Soumya was on his way to the toilet behind the house, which was shared by everyone. The owner of the house and school was up and about already.

But what was this? How could a man beat someone this way with his own hands?

And how could anyone allow himself to be beaten up this way—silently, without protesting?

Perhaps it was the consequence of some mistake or insubordination last night.

Deshmukh sahib was a stickler for discipline. He couldn't tolerate any deviation from the norm. Hadn't Amrita said as much the very first day?

In spite of all his efforts, Soumya could not dismiss the image of Sanjay assaulting Amrita. But he was called into the house a little later.

Laying out a steaming breakfast and a cup of tea on a small table, Amrita had said, 'Here you are. I'm sorry it's late, please excuse me.'

Her eyes were red and swollen. Many years of agony seemed to have gathered in them.

'What about Deshmukh sahib?'

Pointing with her finger, Amrita had said, 'He's gone for a bath.'

There was no such thing as a bathroom hereabouts. Half a wall stood between the area where people bathed and the rest of the world. Would they have run out of money putting up an entire wall? The space was next to the kitchen—it was also where the pitcher of water for drinking water stood.

'Terrible stomach ache, just couldn't get out of bed,' Amrita had said very, very softly.

Soumya hadn't considered it wise to spend any more time with her. Gulping his tea down, he had said thank you and left.

But now, at eleven at night, Soumya recollected the events of the morning in sharp detail.

'You haven't eaten yet,' he told Amrita. 'What about your stomach ache?'

'You think I'd risk another beating by having my meal before he gets home?' Amrita shook with laughter. 'I just couldn't get out of bed in the morning. Kanki-bai isn't here, her son is unwell, and so breakfast wasn't made. The guest was not looked after. And Deshmukh sahib took his revenge on me … I took medicines in the afternoon—but what's the use?'

'What do you mean, what's the use? Aren't you going to see a doctor? Aren't you going to get it treated?'

Amrita rose and switched the TV on. The dance and music on Channel Two had reached a furious pace.

Then she told Soumya, 'You're an outsider, what can I tell you, how much can I tell you, for that matter? I've been having this pain for a month, my stomach's bloated. It hurts to sit. But still, I sit on a chair all day to do my work of looking after the affairs of the school. Deshmukh sahib is forever travelling. The school is a residential one, we have a hundred and ten wild boys, looking after them … if someone has broken a leg, someone else has cracked a bone. The guardians are big businessmen—it's me they'll hold responsible, won't they?

'Two days before you came, the pain had become intense. It was Rajju's birthday. Without warning he invited fifty friends to dinner. I would have to welcome them, I would have to cook for them, or Deshmukh would be humiliated. I was dying as I did all the work. Kanki-bai was here, she knows how many times I vomited while cooking—the sahib doesn't! He doesn't, because he has no need to. He has no need to, because Amrita has nowhere else to go. That has been proved by now. That's what he told me this morning while beating me up, "Go to your parents' home if you want to spend all your time in bed."'

'How do you feel now?' Soumya was virtually whispering.

'The medicine has taken care of the pain, but not of the agony. Even after twelve years together, the person I considered my dearest one understands nothing, doesn't even try to listen to what I have to say. Do you know what hurts? The story of our love was a fairy tale around here fifteen years ago. I'm from Jamnagar; my grandfather is a big businessman there. I was visiting my uncles here when I fell ill, and then I joined the local college. Deshmukh sahib was a prominent student leader—after his BSc he was deeply involved in politics. He began to pursue me relentlessly from the very first day. At eighteen what did I know of caste and creed? I was forced to abandon my home, even my parents and brother. My family turned away from me too. "Come with me, Nazmin," said Deshmukh, "give it all up and come away." Now that the road back is closed to me, I don't even get the respect due to a human being, not even the respect that Kanki-bai commands. Believe me.'

'What was all that about your time running out?' said Soumya. 'Have you any idea of the hardships people endure just to survive?' Just the other day he had seen the state of the people trapped in the water in the valley. The villages would be submerged again in the monsoon. The stars twinkled beyond them, above the distant peaks. The black sky was like soft velvet. There was a moisture-laden wind, and the trees swayed. Fortunately Rajju had fallen asleep. Had her son been awake, how would Amrita or Nazmin have lightened her load? She was standing at the doorstep now, gazing at the narrow trail snaking down the side of the hill.

Coming back into the room, Amrita said, 'No, I guess he's not eating at home. He wouldn't have been so late otherwise.'

'You were talking of the hardships people face, weren't you?'

'I've seen it all when I travelled around with Deshmukh, when he used to take me with him. I've been to rallies in the flooded areas; I've escaped being arrested by the skin of my teeth. And then back home I've had to look after my child and cook for everyone. Theirs is a particular kind of suffering—when entire villages are submerged by the backflow from the dam in the monsoon, when people have to live on planks suspended from trees, without water to drink, snakes everywhere, dead people flowing away on the water … And mine's a different kind, I feel a bleeding inside me every day, in the early hours of the morning I have the urge to walk out of this house …'

'But you didn't walk out, did you!' Soumya's words slipped out. He restrained himself from uttering the remaining words with great effort. Considering this house, a roof, the television, the expensive saris, the jewellery, the food, there was bound to be a difference with the people displaced by the water.

Rajju stirred in his sleep, saying something continuously and unintelligibly in a slurred voice.

Amrita leaned over her son, scanning his face. 'I couldn't do it because of Rajju,' she said. 'His father won't give him up. I couldn't bear to be separated from him all this time. But I've got over it now. Even if I don't get him, even if I cannot see him for six months, a year, still …'

Her eyes brimmed over with tears, her face turned red. Amrita looked at the floor to control her grief.

'This morning my son said, "Go home to your parents, Ma. I can manage, I can stay with Baba, go and get a respite from all this."'

Amrita lowered her voice. Although there was no one nearby, not even an owl. It was nearly midnight. With dark circles under her glittering eyes, she said to Soumya as though telling him a mystery story, 'I got a letter from my brother. My father still doesn't talk to me or write, but he has asked my brother to keep in touch with me. My brother says, "Come whenever you want to. I'll look after you."'

'Will you really abandon such a large school, the hostel, everything? Give it some more time; let the school establish itself …'

A rumbling sound rose in the impenetrable darkness from the other side of the field—soft, but making the heart tremble. Deshmukh's motorcycle had left the highway to climb the unpaved winding trail uphill, like a conspiracy …

'He's coming. Get up now, go to your room …'

Soumya sped across the doorstep like a scalded man before Amrita's slim, fair fingers could touch his shoulder. He couldn't afford to displease Sanjay Deshmukh. He had to write a major report, but the leader had not yet arrived from Indore. Sanjay had the magic wand for arranging a meeting with her. Soumya would go back quickly, spread his mattress out on the floor and lie down on it, feigning deep sleep—of course, he would first have to wrap his head in a thin sheet without a single hole in it, to avoid being bitten by the ants.

Amrita walked across the doorstep too, as though she were disappointed and slighted by Soumya's sudden departure. Perhaps she had expected him not to leave, not to turn his back on her so quickly.

'The elections are in December,' said Amrita. 'I've come to know that Deshmukh will stand in the elections. With me here he'll get votes from both the communities—he planned the whole thing not now but fourteen years ago, which was why he had dangled a bait for a bride from a different religion. I shall leave before the elections are notified, so that he cannot win ...'

Soumya waited no longer. He went into his room before his eyes could be blinded by the headlight of the motorbike, making good his escape.

The roar of the motorbike travelled round and round in his sleep all night. Fear for Amrita and excitement about his own assignment created a thousand pinpricks of light in his head.

The leader arrived in the early hours of the morning.

An eleven-hour bus journey from Indore. The bus was packed with workers involved in the agitation, people from other districts who had been swept away. Surath arrived, and

Dhemni and Bisa Baiga; Dipankar was there, and so were Manoj and Sudipa …

Sanjay Deshmukh had not yet woken up from his whisky-laced slumber. Rajju was asleep.

Soumya took the initiative and introduced himself to the leader of the agitation. A coarse handloom sari, a few strands of grey hair on a brow that had been awake all night, a tired, hoarse voice …

She moved around a wide area like a fireball. Everyone loved her—all these unarmed people were her friends.

Amrita awoke and made black tea for everyone on the bus. The cups were passed around.

Much later, when the sun had risen, the person explained to rows of satyagrahis sitting on the ground how to combat the batons of the police with non-violence. 'You can be beaten, but you must stand erect, hold your head high—you know we have our backs to the wall, you know we have no ground beneath our feet, our battle is with a conspiracy between large farmers, big businessmen and major corporations …'

Medha Patkar's voice floated in the air over the cheap loudspeakers hired by Deshmukh like ground flower petals … 'Upright … stand upright … battle, battle …'

By then Amrita Deshmukh had traversed the sunlit road to reach the bus station in town.

Soumya's detailed report included the history of the agitation, many of the leader's statements, references to Surath, Dhemni and the rest of them. Amrita's face had long been submerged in the human flood.

THE RIGHT TO INFORMATION, OR APRIL 7

When it was time to return home from the office, the hotbox for lunch and the huge circular 'cool jug' of water were the first to leave. Kallol's wife Bratati did not trust the water anywhere on earth. Even bottled water was drawn from ponds these days. She certainly didn't trust people. So, it was boiled water from home. Next to leave were the important documents for the next morning's meetings. A couple of bundles of files too, wrapped in red felt, about thrice a week. On some days he had to spend so much time talking to different people that the files remained unattended.

Kallol had two orderlies of his own. They were the ones who carried all these things out. Then, when told by one of the orderlies that Kallol had risen to his feet, the driver brought the car round to the portico. It did not suit an officer of his weight to be made to wait. No one bothered about such things in Delhi, but it was different at the state level. It was impossible to be effective unless one maintained appearances. So, his private secretary Lalitkumar had told his boss right at the beginning, albeit deferentially, 'Don't leave without warning, sir. Only after I've announced the car.'

In specific situations even the private secretary could not be disobeyed.

Today, too, Kallol had just got to his feet with the intention of returning home as he did every day—the clock said seven-fifteen—when Lalitkumar entered, his face tinged with a trace of tension.

'GM Akhilesh Varma is here.'

'Now?'

'Some important work, he says.'

An irked Kallol resumed his seat. By virtue of his post, he was the chairman of about ten sick, decaying corporations. Akhilesh was the general manager at one of them. A very prudent, experienced, shrewd individual. His unannounced arrival at seven in the evening was as unexpected as it was cause for anxiety. Who knew what had happened. The warehouse hadn't caught fire, had it? Or had the bank seized their account? Maybe there had been a scam with the stock? Several disparate thoughts ran through Kallol's mind immediately. Tomorrow was Saturday. An accident on Friday evening meant a ruined weekend. On top of which, the state legislature was in session. The market for news was bullish. No one knew which item of news could lead to a 'call attention' motion, or which would be converted into a starred question in the Assembly.

'What's the matter, Mr Varma?'

When Kallol was in a good mood he addressed his subordinates by their first name, and by their surnames when he was angry or tense.

Without a word, Varma extended a yellow envelope towards him.

'What's this?'

Varma still didn't speak. He only took a sheet of paper out of the envelope and held it open for Kallol to see.

A notice.

On white paper, of course. Using legal jargon, it said that you are being summoned to the Information Commission on April 7, at ten-thirty a.m., with all relevant information and evidence. And if you do not present yourself ... the commission is free to take any unilateral decision it sees fit.

Kallol took a few seconds to read the letter and decipher its meaning. He had to read more than a hundred different letters every day. About twenty of these were related to court cases. No, his memory had played no tricks in this case, but he found it a little difficult to analyse and digest the fact that the Information Commission had summoned him, Kallol Roychowdhury.

Assuming that he could not remember what it was about, and using his silence as an opportunity, Varma said, 'This is that woman's case, sir, Das's wife ... Tanima Das ...'

There is no need whatsoever to remind me, Kallol thought to himself, for it is impossible to forget either Tanima Das's presence or her letters. The combative wife of a wrongdoer. A departmental enquiry was underway against 'corporation attender' Gopal Das for flouting rules—it had been going on for nearly four years now. The company's hand against corruption had been strengthened after Kallol's arrival, as a result of which police cases had been registered against employees like Gopal Das, with complaints being lodged in the courts for causing deliberate monetary loss and breaking contractual terms. Detractors said this was eyewash. The management had taken on the task of reducing its workforce, the formal term these days being 'rightsizing'; foreign aid would be available only if a hundred people could be taken off the rolls. It wasn't possible to offer Voluntary Retirement Schemes to everyone overnight, and even if it was, not everyone would accept them anyway. So with an iron hand they were trying to sack those who had been accused of corruption or negligence—this lent the rightsizing the fragrance of ethics, while the trade union could not protest and funds for voluntary retirement were saved.

Staff members like Gopal Das earned four thousand rupees a month on average. About one and a half times the earnings of a part-time maid in the city. Kallol broke into a sweat wondering how a man could run his household, educate his children, dress in clean clothes and shave and go to work every day on this salary. As was the case with most of them, some of them ran small businesses on the side to survive, while others resorted to corruption. About six years ago a special audit had led to Gopal Das's being accused of siphoning off twenty-seven thousand rupees. There was a difference of twenty-seven thousand rupees between the official value of the stock in his custody and the auditor's estimate. The departmental enquiry and the police case had been going on ever since. About fifteen other people were snared in a web of similar cases. But none of them had either a malicious mind like Gopal Das's or a luscious wife like Tanima Das. Was it not a glaring example of the discrimination in the world's social infrastructure that a downright poverty-stricken man about to lose his job should have such a committed wife? Even Bratati, the wife of a man as important as Kallol, didn't wait up to eat dinner with him when he was late. If he suddenly needed money, she actually lent him some, saying, 'Here you are, I don't have any more.' What would happen if Kallol's boss were to file two civil cases and one criminal case against him, as he had done against Gopal Das? Wouldn't Bratati split her bed and bank account and move into her own (gifted by Kallol) flat? She definitely would, and she couldn't be blamed for it.

Gopal Das's wife Tanima had been visiting Kallol's office regularly for a couple of years now. Two hours were allocated every Saturday afternoon to listen to public complaints. Tanima used to show up with her applications. Dark-skinned and well-built, she would dress in crumpled handloom saris with her hair tied back, a large teep on her forehead and sindoor in her hair. Lalitkumar had told her a couple of times that taking her application to the GM or even the managing director of the company would be good enough. Kallol was too senior to meet her, too important an officer. As if a company chairman ever entertained such routine complaints! Without being intimidated in the slightest by the weight of Kallol's post, Tanima had said, shaking her head, 'No, I know that he alone can give me justice.'

Initially Tanima Das's handwritten visitor's slip had been swept away in the Saturday crowd and the frequency of visits by the Kanorias, the Garodias and the workers' union. Tanima wasn't the kind of person to add a five- or ten-rupee note to her slip when handing it to the peon.

Even when she wasn't summoned for three hours, she had remained sitting obstinately. Before it was time for Kallol to leave, Lalitkumar and the orderlies had tried what might be referred to as getting rid of her. But Tanima hadn't left. Eventually Kallol had spotted her standing near the wall of the corridor as he was leaving and asked, 'Who is she? Why has she been made to wait so long to present her grievance?'

Kallol had scanned Tanima's appeal right there in the corridor. The content of all her applications had been more or less the same since then.

Gopal Das had not sold any of the stock, he had never had stock of the value mentioned by the auditor, and therefore the company's allegations were incorrect.

Kallol had felt perturbed initially. The accusations had been rejected in clear terms, the quality of English being far from pedestrian. The applicant had waited for several hours without getting an audience. 'Very well, I'll examine this,' he had said. 'I'll let you know if there's anything to be done.'

To the ordinary public, a statement such as this from Kallol's powerful lips was all that was required. But Tanima was different. 'You'll let me know? Through a letter? When?'

'Do you expect sir to commit a date right now?' Lalit had asked angrily.

'All right,' Tanima had answered, 'when should I check again? Next Saturday?'

'Try the Saturday after next.' This was Kallol's attempt to extricate himself by asking for some time.

Normally a fortnight is a long time, especially when the need is one's own. But somehow the days would pass very quickly in the case of Tanima's plea.

The visitor's slip written in the same hand fifteen days later would disturb Kallol as though it were an overt threat.

She was here again! Once more!

'Can you check what's happened to her application,' he would tell Lalit.

'It's nothing to do with this office,' Lalit would answer with a smile. 'It will go to the corporation and be dealt with there. The MD will return it with his comment ...'

'But check anyway, it would have been filed here before it was sent to the corporation ...'

Then it would turn out that the section officer was absent, or the senior clerk was on leave. In other words, there was no information for Tanima.

Tanima would appear and stand in silence.

Kallol would be annoyed. He felt naked, unarmed. 'It hasn't come back to me yet. Once it does, I can explain the situation.'

'When should I come then? Next Saturday?'

'All right.'

It would be the same story the next Saturday.

Kallol did not know at first that there would be so many applications on Grievance Day. All of them were left in bundles—none of them was put up to anyone in files.

Later, his helplessness would be converted to rage.

Tanima, Tanima and even more of Tanima. Every Saturday.

He would telephone Varma and Chaubey, the MD, to express his unhappiness.

'Why don't you comment on the grievance petition? It's not been sent back to me yet.'

They would express polite, deferential surprise.

'Did you send something, sir? I'll check. But Das's case is under progress. It's been four years. We've lodged an FIR.'

One day Kallol had told Tanima with angry eyes, 'Don't keep coming back, Mrs Das. You know the case is sub judice.'

'I'm not here about the court case,' Tanima had said in surprise. 'I'm here about the departmental enquiry. Nothing prevents me from making a complaint, does it?'

'Fine, then keep coming back.'

'I have presented fifteen applications till now. None of them has been answered. You are the chairman of the corporation. If you don't have the answer, what can your subordinates do?'

'I don't know. Nor am I obliged to answer. Please don't disturb me every day, don't waste my time.'

Kallol's voice had become louder. One of the orderlies rushed in. He hadn't meant to throw it, but still a paperweight had slipped from his hand and shattered the glass on a low table next to the desk.

Tanima stopped her Saturday visits after this. Kallol was somewhat contrite, but relieved.

There was work, pressure and tension all week. But in spite of all this, waiting for Tanima every Saturday had become something of a habit—there was a powerful manliness in rejecting her. When she stopped coming, Tanima deprived Kallol of his weekly pleasure, but rid him of his anxiety too.

Kallol hadn't realised that things had taken a different turn.

Chaubey the MD phoned him one day. He was a quiet, fearful, plump man, not a sly fox like Akhilesh Varma. He never took the initiative. But this time he was anxiously passing on the news to Kallol.

'Tanima Das has filed an application under the Information Act, sir, asking for lots of documents.'

Kallol was astonished. It had barely been a year since the Information Act had been passed, and the workers and officers had only just been trained for it—how to ensure that people had the right to information. Kallol himself had written a couple of articles, attended training seminars and brainwashed his staff into believing that information was the primary basis of democracy. But still, Tanima's application under the Information Act was unexpected!

'That woman is quite something!' observed Lalit. 'Gopal is just a dummy, hiding behind his wife and watching the fun.'

'What documents has Tanima Das asked for? Let me see the application.'

Chaubey seemed utterly demoralised. 'She has asked for entire sets of documents. A long list of twenty-one sets of documents in all. Starting with the audit report all the way to office correspondence. How can we give her all this?'

'Don't even bother, sir,' said Lalit. 'The Act lists the kind of information that need not be provided. Chaubey is the first officer of appeal, he will reject the application.'

Hesitating, Kallol said, 'What harm will it do to provide the information? Can you bring me a copy of the Act, please?'

They sat around a table with copies of the Act—the office lawyer, Chaubey, Varma, Lalit. With coffee, paneer pakoras and prawn cutlets. They began to underline the relevant parts.

Section Eight of the Information Act listed the kind of information that need not be provided …

Information that could compromise the safety and security of the country
Information that would invade the privacy of an individual
Information pertaining to confidential ministerial discussions

In this manner, as they read through the sections, there it was!

If providing information during an enquiry could hamper it, those in possession of the information are not bound to disclose it.

Clearing his throat, Kallol said, '... But they can provide it too, can't they? On the flip side of every "need not provide" there's also a "may provide", isn't there?'

Varma, Chaubey and Lalit were all astonished, but they didn't want to say anything, keeping in mind the gap between their respective positions and Kallol's.

Who knew whether the boss was joking, or whether he was serious, or whether he was simply trying to gauge their stance?

Actually, as they read Section Eight, an image floated up in Kallol's mind through the gaps in the letters—of Aruna Roy. The leader of the movement for the right to information. When he had joined the administration during his involvement with leftist student politics, he had said as an excuse, how will I change everything unless I'm an insider? His university friends had laughed so loudly that he had spilt his tea and scalded his knee. This agony was compounded by the twenty-three-year-old Kallol's rage. These people are asses. They'll be clerks all their lives, they will be penpushers, but they will never understand what ambition is. There was no biotechnology, no MTechs or MBAs, not even a whiff of software in the air back then.

Nineteen seventy-eight.

The Left Front had come to power in West Bengal. Kallol and his friends had marched in victory parades. Left leaders who had had to go underground were emerging into the open.

People were streaming out on the roads. Everyone from the bus conductor to the water carrier was a 'comrade'. Still fired by this dream, Kallol had scored a jackpot in the all-India examination and gone for training. Then, when he was posted in a small sub-divisional town, he began to work with the ferocity of a lion. It was at this time that Aruna Roy had paid a visit. When he went back home one evening, he discovered his bodyguards trying their best to explain to a woman in a white sari with a brown border, her hair uncombed, her appearance dishevelled, 'Go back, madam, sir doesn't meet anyone at home at this hour ...'

Kallol was overwhelmed. By this sudden visit on Aruna's part during her tour, the activist and the young sub-divisional officer sharing khichuri for dinner. With curd, pickles and papad. Aruna had told him about her experience of working with the poorest of the poor in Rajasthan; of her movement, ten years later, for the right to information, organising people, winning the Magsaysay ... At a seminar on the Information Act, Kallol had declared proudly, 'I know the person whose movement and sensitivity to people's needs made this Act possible ... Aruna Roy ...'

As Kallol read Section Eight of the Act, the image of his meal with Aruna rose before his eyes. But the people sitting in front of him appeared far more clearly than Aruna.

Tanima's application was rejected under Section Eight, Sub-section H. Information Officer Varma's instructions were recorded on the file. What was referred to as a 'speaking order'. Tanima lodged an appeal, filling in all the relevant details in the form and paying the requisite fees. This time she was rejected by Chaubey. The next appeal was to Kallol. When he received the application, a part of his heart kept saying, why not provide the documents—what difference would it make? The departmental enquiry had ended. A second and final show-cause notice had been issued to Gopal Das. He had no hope. Providing the information was unlikely to hamper anything.

But Kallol was no longer the Kallol of 1978—his hands were no longer tinged with the red gulal of victory. He was not even an individual anymore. He was an institution. Hundreds of people were dependent on him. Any weakness on his part would now lower the standing of the institution. Chaubey, Varma, Prasad, Kumar, Lahiri and the rest raised such a hue and cry—labelling his intrinsic weakness a case of casting pearls before undeserving and poor swine—that Tanima Das's second appeal was also rejected by Kallol's own hand.

All this had happened about three months ago.

Now, after all the other work and incidents that had taken place since then, Kallol seemed to be searching for his own existence again in the rerun of his memory triggered by the information commissioner's summons.

The entire sequence of events came back to him. Tanima's Saturday visits. The application to the grievance cell. Tanima waiting. The paperweight slipping out of his fingers and shattering the glass on the low table next to the desk. A woman had stalked Kallol like a hunter for a year now.

Kallol observed Varma's cold, cruel face. Tucking the yellow envelope between the pages of a diary, he was staring fixedly at Kallol. His eyelids didn't drop, as though he were a reptile. Varma looked as though he would lay down his life to fulfil Kallol's wishes.

'So I have to show up on April 7.' Kallol smothered a sigh. 'What if I don't go? Will they issue a ruling unilaterally?'

'No, you should go, sir. Why should it be unilateral? You shall go with your head held high, we're making arrangements.'

Summoning Lalitkumar, Kallol said, 'The commission doesn't have its own building yet. Can you find out where the sittings are being held? Since I have to go.' Strangely, this man Gopal Das had only sent his wife all this time. He had never come himself.

What Varma said with his eyes on the floor amounted to this: these kamina men, these bastards, always try to fool us with their tricks.

Kallol hadn't been to the courts very often. In his entire life he had had to go to the High Court a couple of times on charges of contempt of court, but that was all. The chief information commissioner was a retired colleague—he needn't fear a threat or humiliation. Kallol tried to reassure himself. But still he appeared irritable and crotchety—to Bratati. A suppressed tension had made him fidget all day.

The administrative section of town was always spick and span. At about ten-twenty on the morning of April 7, his driver Sadashiva left the main road and drove all the way up and down the road that crossed it at right angles. Lalitkumar had given the address to Sadashiva and not to Kallol. The man was going round in circles like a fool. The hearing was at ten-thirty. Kallol was annoyed—he didn't like being late. Especially in such situations, when he was the one under fire.

'Stop the car,' said Kallol suddenly, loudly.

He had spotted Tanima Das near a gate, standing almost like a statue. Immediately afterwards he noticed the board with the name of the commission. Kallol didn't know, but the day before yesterday—on April 5, in other words—Gopal Das had been terminated from his job. According to an order from Chaubey. Tanima had refused to receive the dismissal notice at home. So, today, on April 7, the dismissal notice had been printed in the local newspaper, with Gopal Das's photograph. Royal arrangements for the social humiliation of Gopal Das, the criminal.

Kallol would have noticed it himself had his mind not been wandering.

A simple soul and a little religious, Chaubey had been hesitant initially. Gopal Das had been bedridden for a year. He wasn't getting paid anyway. Was it really necessary to drive the last nail in the coffin? The shortage was of twenty-seven thousand rupees only. Nothing compared to what the Telgis and their ilk had done. Akhilesh Varma the reptile had put immense pressure on Chaubey. 'That's hardly the issue, sir. This is a matter of the chairman's prestige. Doesn't he have to go to the commission with his head held high? Throw the traitor out.'

Eventually Chaubey did release the termination order. Kallol didn't even come to know that his cohorts had changed him instead of changing the rubric of democracy.

Rolling up the dark windows of his car, Kallol told Sadashiva to turn the air conditioner up. It was a short journey to the gate, but he wasn't going to travel fuming.

Tanima Das didn't look at him. She stood as though she had been turned to stone.

Was it Tanima, or Aruna? The figure was blurred at this distance.

THE LAST SAMURAI

When Brata reached the landing on the first-floor staircase, he found his student ready to go out. Her hair done in a ponytail, she was dressed in jeans and a T-shirt, and shoes with matching socks. When she saw Brata, she began to jump down the stairs. Brata had practically run all the way from the bus stop—his shirt was stuck to his back with perspiration. 'Where are you going?' he asked.

Maani paid no attention to the question. Instead, she shouted, 'Yojimbo Takashi Shimura Tora Tora Tora,' and leapt down the last three steps.

Just imagine! Thank goodness Brata had managed to grab her, or else she would have fallen on her face.

'How can you just jump without looking?' Brata tried to scold her mildly and attempted to set her on her feet.

Maani wrapped her arms and legs around him and said, mussing his hair, 'Tora Tora Tora … heeheehee.'

'Misbehaving again, Maani?' her mother Rina was heard saying at the top of the stairs.

'I'm speaking in Japanese with Kaku.'

Brata felt the muscles of his shoulder and neck stiffening even before Maani had answered. The same thing had happened while speaking to Maani's father on the phone from the office a short while ago. His physical reactions began before his body was aware of them.

'Oh no, we should have telephoned you … actually we just decided to visit her grandmother …' said Rina, parting her dark burgundy lips. Her eyes couldn't be read behind her sunglasses. 'You can't do that, Maani, get down at once.'

Maani jumped out of Brata's arms. Not because of her mother, but because her father was upstairs too. Sugata smiled at Brata. The smile held no significance, which was why Brata's expression did not change.

Touching his wife lightly on the back and walking down the stairs with his daughter, Sugata repeated what Rina had said …

'We really should have telephoned you.'

Sugata's smile had made it obvious to Brata that even Rina did not know about the phone call made earlier. Perhaps no one would ever know.

Brata stood by himself for some time after they had left. There was a bench that he could sit on. Door-to-door salesgirls often used it for a spot of rest in the afternoons. Or chauffeurs. It would look strange for Brata to sit there. Through the glass window, he could see the mango tree swaying in the wind. A solitary crow kept flitting between its branches. Like a persistent fever, the humiliation that Sugata had heaped on him refused to leave. Although Rina and Maani didn't know, Brata felt no relief at this.

It was Maani's birthday. Brata had brought two books for her—one English and one Bengali. He hadn't been able to give them to her—hadn't been able to wish her either, for they had left very quickly. Brata had not expected Sugata to be back home so soon—but he should have.

On other days, Sugata played bridge for several hours at the office after work. Obviously he wouldn't do it on his daughter's birthday! When Maani went back home from school, Rina gave her something to eat and then went out in the car. She had many engagements. Swimming classes. Baking and Chinese lessons twice a week. Not that Brata and Maani had a problem if Rina didn't go out. He could read to her. They could talk in code language. They could even converse in Bangla provided they kept their voices low.

When Maani got particularly excited, she spoke very loudly, waving her arms and legs, or laughed at the top of her voice.

If Rina were at home at the time, her voice wafted out along with the scent of toasted bread ...

'Are you misbehaving again, Maani!'

'No, Ma, no, Mummy,' Maani would say, running up to her and butting her midriff with her head.

If her mother got angry, she phoned her father. Her father came home and scolded Maani in English.

Speaking in English was compulsory in Maani's school. From the moment they entered the school premises till they left. The class monitors checked whether anyone was talking in a different language. They complained to the teachers, and the students were fined. Rina kept small change handy these days. Maani took one rupee and fifty paise to school on some days, three rupees and seventy-five paise on others. Two boys named Shailu and Preetam spoke in a torrent of Hindi to each other. Maani, Sujata and Ankit spoke in Bengali stealthily. The monitor's name was Gaautum (Gautam) Baus (Bose). Very sly, forever skulking near Maani and her friends. At first the school used to impose large fines—the principal had even sent for Sugata once. Sugata had beaten Maani mercilessly. She was such a pet of his, he brought her gifts and her favourite food all the time, and yet what a terrible beating he had given her!

'She won't mend her ways without a beating,' Sugata had declared, panting. 'Have you any idea of the things I had to do getting her admitted? Do you suppose it's easy to get into this school?'

The beating had given Maani a fever.

Rina shivered when she remembered.

Now, mother and girl had come to some sort of agreement. Rina could take care of small fines of up to five rupees. Sugata didn't have to be informed. She took the money out of the jar on top of the fridge without Sugata finding out.

Sugata had slapped Rina no more than once or twice. He was a terror when he drank. The marks had been concealed under expensive cottons and chiffons. Rina's family didn't know.

Brata's office operated with two shifts—one from eight in the morning till three in the afternoon, and the other from three till about ten. Brata went to work on the morning shift. It was a firm of middlemen, a consultancy for foreign trade, buying and selling of licences. Brata was new here. His tasks were relatively unimportant. He didn't have to dispense suggestions or advice; no clients' files were stacked in his cupboard. Brata didn't even have a cupboard yet. Perched on a backless stool for hours on end, he noted down details of the work done by the firm in notebooks or entered data at a computer terminal. Churiwal, the owner of the firm, gave him a couple of casual assignments once in a while. 'This will do for now,' one of his elder brothers had told him. 'If you get a better job afterwards ...'

Brata's BA results in Economics hadn't been bad, but he had hit a roadblock at 54 per cent in the MA examinations. He took the entrance test for banks twice, failing both times. After doing the morning shopping for the family, Brata roamed about all afternoon, following in the wastrel-like footsteps of his elder brother. The job fell into his hands at this time like a plum.

The environment was ugly, there was filth in every pore of the work he did, but Brata had no other option right now. Meanwhile, a call came from Rina via his sister-in-law. Rina was tired of staying home all day. She was beautiful, noble, smart. There were so many things she wanted to do. But Sugata wouldn't let her leave their daughter home and go out. It displeased him. Maani went to a very good school. She had loads of homework, dozens of sums, social science, geography ... who was going to get all this done?

A wonderful balancing act had taken place between Brata's shift at work and Rina's desire to spread her wings—in terms of time. Leaving his office around three-fifteen, Brata reached Ballygunge Circular Road by four o'clock. Rina went out at four-fifteen, returning at six-thirty. In case she was late, Brata had to leave after informing their maid Shyama.

His elder brothers had not been pleased. 'This is nothing but babysitting,' they had said. 'She's getting you to look after the child because she can't trust the maid.'

Maybe. During these two hours or so Brata made Maani do her homework, told her stories, got her to draw and ... taught her the Bengali alphabet on the sly. Besides, there was their code language. Right now, it was Japanese. Spouting meaningless, made-up words. 'Call him sir, not Kaku ...' and 'Control yourself, Maani,' were a constant refrain that both of them had to hear. Every time he heard either of these, his shoulder and neck muscles stiffened. He wasn't inclined to glance at Rina's polished, gleaming face.

No, Brata wouldn't be able to give Maani up. The girl had wound herself around him. This was a completely different kind of bond for the twenty-six-year-old Brata. He was aware that his sister-in-law shielded her son from his jobless uncle, not allowing them to spend much time together. Bablu, who was younger than Maani, was much more practical, much more restrained. When Brata brought him a gift, he didn't snatch it from his hands, accepting it placidly and saying thank you. If he needed anything unusual for a school project, he told Brata, 'Can you get it from somewhere near your office?'

Maani, plump and round, was completely different. Shyama used to keep an eye on them initially, passing through the room several times on the pretext of doing her chores. A man, after all. They could never be trusted entirely. Brata would turn red, knowing that he was being kept under surveillance. Nowadays Shyama napped contentedly after giving him a cup of tea and something to eat. She even went out to get the milk and to buy vegetables from the nearby store.

Whenever Shyama was out of sight Maani looked around furtively and then climbed onto Brata's lap. And proceeded to complete her tasks as though this was her rightful place. She tousled his hair. He set her down when it was time for her to write.

At seven and a half, the girl still smelt of infant milk. Her hair covered her brow and fell on her eyes. Her body was perpetually cool and moist with perspiration. One moment she'd be eating something, the next she'd wipe her fingers on Brata's cheek, leaving it sticky. The child was so desperate for touch, so hungry for affection. She had to behave in a restrained fashion in the presence of her parents—her mother pushed Maani away lightly when the child went near her, for fear of crumpling her sari. She had to give her father a bye-bye kiss when he left for office in the morning. On the days that Sugata left before her, he bent to hold his cheek out to her. The scent of after-shave kept Maani at a distance.

Doitter Ketli. The Ogre's Kettle. Maani was very amused by the title. She laughed loudly, for there was no one at home, before beginning the book from the middle. At school it was all English. A little Hindi alongside. No one had taught her Bengali. Sugata had already warned Rina strongly. He had not forgotten all the effort he had been forced to put in to conceal his background as a student of the Bengali-medium school Manindrachandra Vidyapeeth. The smile that appeared on his colleagues' lips at this Bengali-accented English had not escaped his observation. Sugata wouldn't allow his child to tread this path of humiliation. Which was why Maani and Brata hid *The Ogre's Kettle* among the termite-ridden newspapers, chunks of wood and other rubbish on the lowest rack of the wardrobe, along with *Chhelebyalar Dinguli* and a tattered copy of *Holdey Pakhir Palok*—all of them prizes that Brata had won in school. Their enormous notebook and box of colour pencils lay in silence amidst these. On every page were written Bengali words with conjoint letters in a large hand—jawtno, rawtno, petni, khokkhosh—which Maani complained loudly about as she read them, shaking her head.

'Why did you set me such hard words to spell?' she shouted. 'Just you wait, I'll bite you.' And she really did sink her teeth into his arms through the shirt sleeves. Maani had learnt much of the Bengali alphabet this way in secret in the past three months—with many conjoint letters among them. Neither Rina nor Sugata had an inkling.

Brata had filled the pages of the large interleaved notebook with Bengali letters. He had a knack for drawing. Maani coloured inside the outlines with the pencils. Then the letters were cut out with scissors and put in a file. They wouldn't be pasted on the wall. These letters would not be glued on the walls of this house with plastic paint on them. Never. Brata knew. But still they went on. Brata was consumed by his addiction to the game of taking Maani down an unknown path without Sugata and Rina's knowledge.

Sugata hadn't phoned him at home. Did he know already that Brata wasn't himself in office? On his chair without a backrest, he was terrified, a spineless coward. Having taken Brata's number from his brother, Sugata had practically skinned him alive over the phone for seven minutes. Brata was unfamiliar with this booming, blunt voice of Sugata's.

'You get paid, you tutor the child, just teach her what you're being asked to … black holes, nebulae, Orion—what's all this? Did you read science in college? You didn't? Economics wasn't enough for you, obviously! Why are you telling her things you know nothing about? Filling a little girl's head with trash—blood and bone cancer rates are up in Pokhran? You know more than nuclear scientists? Tomorrow onwards, Rina will tell you what you have to teach—my wife! Forget all this Cuba and Namibia business. If you're up to it, find college students to teach—no one will stop you. Why are you trying to ruin a child of seven?'

Brata's throat was dry. At Sugata's unexpected attack and the hostile atmosphere. Brata couldn't get himself to offer a logical argument, although he knew that Sugata must have rehearsed the text of his assault meticulously. Had Maani revealed everything to her father? Maybe she had waltzed up to him with the scrapbook in which Brata pasted national and international news items clipped from newspapers and magazines. He explained these events in simple terms to Maani. Both Rina and Sugata were delighted about the nuclear tests, but Brata hadn't been able to hold back from telling Maani what he thought. Did this amount to ruining her? Samaresh-jethu had given Brata *The Hunchback of Notre Dame* when he was eight; he had read *Durgeshnandini* when in Class Five. Had he been led astray? Maani's eager, restless air calmed Brata down every time. No, he hadn't made a mistake—the girl listened to every word. He didn't know how much she understood, but Brata had no doubt that she was equally attracted by the earth with its land and water and the sky with its stars.

Sugata had disconnected the phone without giving Brata a chance to say anything. Brata had reached Maani's home at four as usual, assuming that Sugata would be in office at that hour. He didn't have a clear notion of what kind of exchange they would have if they ran into each other. An icy feeling made his insides shrink now and then. Maani and her parents went out, unconcerned. All that Sugata said was, 'We really should have just telephoned you.' Extraordinary man! As though nothing had happened. As though Brata had not been subjected to a tirade a short while ago. Was he a doormat which would lie in silence even if people scraped their dirty feet on it?

No, not another day here. Putting away the book meant for Maani, Brata vanished. One day, two days, three days passed—Brata didn't go to Maani's house after work. He went to Victoria Memorial on one of those days, and to Max Mueller Bhavan on the other two. It was impossible to forget Maani's cool cheeks or her laughter—which sounded like falling water—or the way she plopped on his lap. The spoilt child of rich parents, she would forget everything in a couple of days with some bubblegum and ice-cream. Telling himself all this, a stricken Brata forced Maani's image away from his mind. But she refused to go away. Pouncing on him, she tousled his hair, saying, 'Tora Tora Tora … heeheehee!'

Rina telephoned him early one morning. Anxious, a little displeased too. 'What's the matter? You haven't been coming. Maani's almost stopped eating. You could have informed us. Aren't you well?' When he rang the doorbell at Maani's house that afternoon, someone threw herself at the door to open it. And then Maani, dressed in a sleeveless T-shirt and Bermuda shorts, turned her back to him and walked away.

Her lips frosted in preparation for going out, Rina said, smiling, 'She's angry with you, she's a child after all. She would stand outside at the door at four o'clock every day.'

Maani had hidden herself behind the door. But with one arm and one leg quite visible, so that Brata would have no trouble finding her. Running up to her, Brata took her hand and led her to the study. Instead of sitting on his lap as usual, Maani stood stiffly. Tears streamed from her eyes, moistening the back of her hands. Brata's heart burst with love. He whispered to her …

'Monogatari hawn?'

Code for: Want a story?

'Monogatari nawn,' replied Maani, her voice wet with tears.

No, don't want.

If Yasujiro Ozu's *Tokyo Monogatari* was *Tokyo Story*, they could certainly work out a Japanese code for 'story', couldn't they? And so 'monogatari' meant 'story'—in their tongue! With the sun out after three cloudy days, the two friends were now thick as thieves. Maani had got a C on her homework for two successive days, which led to some bickering. Then it was back to whispering and giggling. Bringing him something to eat, Shyama said, 'Cloudy one moment, rainy the next! It's a good life!'

He had to tell Maani the story of *Seven Samurai* again. And not quietly, sitting in a chair, but by acting it out. Brata turned into Toshiro Mifune—springing like a leopard and falling to the ground, scratching the ground with his feet like a wild rooster. Three days of accumulated fatigue dropped away from his body like the bark dropping from a tree trunk. So much commercial cinema all around, so many TV channels—how was Maani to fend off bad films unless she saw good ones, how was her taste to develop? Brata had said as much to Rina one day, mildly.

'What can we do?' Rina had smiled. 'That's what everyone watches, all the students in her class sing the latest film songs, practise the dances …'

'Should I try? May I?' Brata had said.

That was how Satyajit Ray's *Pather Panchali* had entered this house, *Agantuk* and *Shakha Proshakha*, too. Brata had rented the video cassettes cheaply from his neighbourhood video store. He had not expected Maani to be interested in *Pather Panchali*, but she had watched the film open-mouthed. When Indir Thakrun died and, later, when Durga fell ill, she had clutched Brata's hand in a storm of emotion. Experiment successful. Congratulations!

Brata patted himself on the back mentally. After this he brought *Seven Samurai*. Akira Kurosawa's film. Impossible to get hold of. The shopkeeper saluted respectfully on hearing the name. Brata turned to a friend of his brother's to make a recording from the original video. One evening, while Sugata and Rina were at the movies, Maani and Brata watched the entire film.

The battle between famished villagers and robbers in the barley fields … with the starving samurai on the side of the villagers … they had come not to extort money but to change the course of events … legendary Japanese actor Toshiro Mifune in the role of the seventh samurai Kikuchiyo! What acting, what expressions, what tension! When Brata saw Maani's shining eyes, he knew this girl wasn't just another girl—she was pure gold! This tree could reach up to the sky. And how wonderful—the girl seemed to absorb whatever Brata offered her all the way down to her roots. So eager! There was so much life in her!

Brata had to transform himself into Toshiro Mifune as compensation for three days' absence. Maani watched him with wide eyes. Rina arrived to scold her mildly. They hadn't done the day's homework yet. You'll get a C again, rightly served. Unwillingly Maani brought her textbooks. When Brata left, Rina said loudly from the balcony, 'Please don't disappear again, come regularly.'

'Yes …' As he was about to smile and wave, Brata realised that the breeze had borne his words away, for Sugata's blue Maruti was approaching him through the darkness like a bad intention. 'All well?' Brata smiled at Sugata, who felt no need to respond.

His sister-in-law had said, 'Find someone else to tutor, Brata, you're getting too enmeshed with this family. The girl's their daughter; she'll be brought up according to their wishes. Rina was saying Sugata isn't happy with what you teach her …'

She didn't bring him a cup of tea every day, but she had that day. Putting the cup down on the table without a sound, Brata had stretched out on the bed.

'I do my best … I don't know!' A hint was enough for the intelligent. Brata would quit. Maybe he could visit Maani now and then. This was such a strange addiction. Private tutors had no business getting into such situations. Why this visceral bond with Maani? Like with one's own child. How odd! He wasn't even married, and here he was thinking of children. Brata felt like laughing and crying at the same time.

Eventually the bird had to fly away from the tree in flames. But its soul remained in the fire, burning, burning. It left, but found no release. There was no escape for the bird. The defeated man had no dreams, only a state of bondage.

About a month later, Brata woke up in a state of melancholy one winter morning. To be precise, he read the news in the papers as soon as he awoke.

Toshiro Mifune had died.

The seventh samurai had left. The man who had acquired his acting prowess one drop at a time from nature, from humanity, from the earth, to leave it all behind in his films for his audiences would no longer be seen on the screen. He was reminded of Maani's face suddenly—a wave crashed on his heart. Had the bridge between them just collapsed?

Breakfast amounted to bread and milk. Following the meal, he went to the office to discover an explosive Churiwal on the rampage. Someone or the other had not saved the data entered into the computer last night, and everything had been lost. It was the fault of the young man named Ajit—but Brata sat down glumly to redo yesterday's work. What would Churiwal say if he mentioned Toshiro Mifune? Kya karta thha woh aadmi? What did that man do? No one here had heard of Akira Kurosawa or seen Satyajit Ray's films. No one talked of Rabindranath Tagore or Jibanananda Das. Brata would have to keep working here till he got something better … keeping his body submerged, he would have to keep his nose above water to breathe.

When he left office, Brata bought an English newspaper. This particular paper gave a little extra coverage to art and culture. It seemed excessive on other days, but today he decided to show Maani both the photograph and the report. He would just show them to her—that's all. No stories, Brata warned himself. Maani's second-term exams were coming up.

Sugata opened the door. Hadn't he gone to office? That familiar expression—he had probably insulted Brata on the phone with a similar expression on his face. Sugata turned and went inside the flat without a word. Brata followed him. The cupboard in the study was open. Papers and books were scattered on the ground. From beneath them Maani and Brata's entire hidden cache had come out in the open—storybooks, music cassettes, the notebook for the Bengali alphabet, the colour pencils ...

'Where's Maani?' Brata's voice sounded like a wounded cry to his own ears.

There was a sound like a caged tiger on the other side of the door.

'Ka...ku!' With a sharp cry Maani freed herself from her mother's grasp and flung herself on Brata.

Her eyes were red and swollen, her expression seemed to have changed in a day. Maani had grown up. She understood everything now.

'They won't let you come anymore.'

'Shut up! No drama!'

Sugata exploded like a bomb.

'So, this is how you study! You, sir, will behave like a madman—and I will pay fines to my daughter's school, right? I live with the enemy!'

As soon as he held up the interleaved notebook, the letters were showered on the red carpet.

There they were, all the conjoint letters—how much effort they had put into colouring them all, Brata and Maani! The letters lay still on the floor like corpses now.

'What are you doing?' Rina came into the room, distraught. 'There's no need to insult him. He needn't teach Maani anymore. I'll stay home, take care of our daughter, but that doesn't mean you ...' Sugata looked at Rina, his eyes immobile.

'Who'll pay for the damage he has done all this time. Will you? The girl is about to lose her entire orientation—she's not interested in studies, her mind is on cinema, on the mysteries of the cosmos. It was only when I went looking for my passbook that I discovered all this. You had an inkling, Rina, but despite being her mother you didn't say anything … very well, I'm sorry, I didn't mean to hurt you, Brata-babu, but no more … if Rina can't do it, I'll take leave till I find a proper tutor …'

'… Look,' clearing his throat, Brata said with great effort, 'I haven't done Maani any harm. I tried to give her what I didn't get myself as a child—your daughter has such a lovely, receptive mind … never mind, let her grow older, you can decide for yourself then whether I was wrong …'

A little later everyone sat down for a cup of excellent Darjeeling tea and coconut cookies. Like a conversation on a tranquil winter evening. Maani's tears had dried. There were biscuit crumbs on her mouth and in her lap. Dabbing them away with a napkin, Sugata said, 'You know what? One has to rise above the limitations of one's class—or else death is inevitable. My father was a refugee. I studied in a Bengali-medium school. Some school that was—we had to sit on the floor till Class Four. But I have managed to rise above all that and move into a higher orbit. The girl goes to a good school, what use is it to teach her the Bengali alphabet? And all this Ray and Kurosawa of yours—but where do you stand today, Brata-babu? A semi-educated Baniya, a hawala trader, can shout at you. Your office chair doesn't even have a backrest. Please don't drag Maani down …'

Brata raised his face sharply, discovering Rina lowering hers in embarrassment, while Maani looked on in surprise.

'Why doesn't the chair have a backrest, Bapi?'

'You needn't know,' said Sugata with a smile.

Brata had to accept his salary for the yet-to-be-completed month in a beautiful envelope. Maani walked him to the door, but with her father behind her, she didn't clutch at Brata's shirt today. 'By the way'—Brata's voice changed to an unfamiliar pitch as he was about to exit—'may I visit Maani sometimes ...?'

'No.' Sugata delivered his verdict speedily. Succinctly. Without explanation. 'Absolutely not. Never.'

Downstairs, Brata looked up at the balcony and spotted Maani. Without her parents. She was waving. Smiling. The implication of Brata's departure was still not clear to her. Trudging through the mist like a blind man, Brata heard Maani's high-pitched voice.

'Ka...ku! Arigato gozaimasu! Arigato ...'

Thank you! Thank you! That was what Maani was saying in code. They used to say 'thank you' between themselves after they watched *Seven Samurai*. Brata hadn't told Maani about Toshiro Mifune's death. Let Mifune remain alive and glowing in a child's mind for some time more.

Every step that Brata took was agony. He felt as though the letters he had drawn with his own hand were scattered all over the road, and that he was trampling on them.

IN THE MOONLIGHT

So, you can't sleep? So what. It's barely a quarter past one at night. And besides, there's no such thing as night in this city. This is Mumbai. It's always daytime here—it's just a matter of degree, so to speak.

Too much noise. Oh, but the rattling trams and honking buses and deafening marketplaces of Calcutta don't seem to bother you. Just try sleeping in the areas around Hazra Road or Shyambazar, AJC Bose Road or Central Avenue and see what happens.

True, you're used to those places. Mumbai is a new city. An unfamiliar flat, a bed you've never slept in. On top of which, all this noise—that too after midnight. How will you sleep? Ten days' vacation, with the days spent gallivanting around the city. You get back to your friend's flat only at night. Never mind, you can sleep soundly after you get back to Calcutta. For now, just try to listen to each of the distinct sounds.

There, the rustling on the rain shade outside the window—even amidst all the hullaballoo, it makes you tremble. Oh yes! That's our lame crow foraging for food. It can't fight with the other strong and greedy crows all day. They scuffle with this one and take away the best bits. But there are always some leftovers, which they cannot spot even in daylight. The lame crow sniffs around for these pieces and brings all of them here to eat them. Can you hear the sound of its dragging its foot? There are very few houses in this area where it isn't shooed away.

Uff! This continuous sobbing—and then the sounds of a wailing quarrel. Horrible. Barking and yowling, a bunch of dogs are wrangling, bickering and fighting at the entrance to the Asha Nagar slum. The Asha Nagar slum? Don't you know it's directly beneath this building? No, you can't see it from this height—nor from the street. How is that possible? It is because this city is run by the Mumbai Mahanagarpalika, or Municipal Corporation, not by the one in Calcutta. Directly beneath the eight fourteen-storeyed towers, concealed behind shiny steel barricades, the slum has seemingly been tucked into the basement. It can't be seen, but women and girls stream out of its belly every day to perform all the chores at the flats in the towers. Advertisements for 'a clean, green and beautiful' Mumbai are pasted on the barricades. Passers-by and VIPs in their cars can only see these images, not the slum or its inhabitants—thanks to the prowess of the Mumbai Mahanagarpalika. Even a few months ago, Leela, too, used to live in this slum. Who's Leela? Really—you're in Mumbai to write a screenplay, and you don't even know the name of the main character? Who do you think? The woman in the churidar-kameez who made your hot rotis in the evening, that's who. You relished the lau kofta she made. She really is a terrific cook. With the alu raita on the side. She served you a couple of pieces of fried pabda fish too. But see, you don't even know her name. Anyway. Let me tell you about the dogs now. NGOs and animal lovers are very powerful in the city of Mumbai. So, killing dogs is not allowed here—not even surreptitiously. The Mahanagarpalika would have had no choice but to allow their tribe to increase. But taking away the dogs in groups under the supervision of NGOs, neutering them and releasing them in the same area is legal. That's what the municipality does. So, these are all neutered dogs. Witness to the death of their own desire and unable to understand the resultant changes in themselves, they have turned into bad-tempered, quarrelsome and confused creatures. They can see the bitches around, but, realising that their bodies are not responding, their intelligence is blunted even more. They bark in different ways—their hunger, the stones that are hurled at them, the kicks—these intense sensations blend with their scraped-off sexuality. They will howl this way till the moon is low and the sky starts lightening. Then the dogs will lie down on the cool pavements, tucking their noses into their paws, and fall asleep. It's the same every day, yes. There's nothing to be done. Nothing at all. Even the enormously powerful Shiv Sena supremo Bal Thackeray was forced to complain to the Shiv Sena, which runs the municipality, that he was unable to sleep for nights on end because of the dogs. It did not help. The dogs were spirited away for a few days, but they came back.

For a while, put aside the howling of the dogs and listen closely. You will reach the second level of sounds. The wheels of the red buses, the rattling of the taxis, the vrooming of sports bikes, the uproar of drunks from a loaded truck or two. This is the regular racket of the city at night—which your Calcutta, too, has—although the heady sound of the sports bikes is absolutely out of place on Calcutta's dilapidated roads. Beyond this level is a third one, which Calcutta does not possess. Pluck yourself out of your bed like a thorn and go strai...ght down to the level of this sound. Well? Can you hear it? Like the roar of a crouching tiger, but in syncopated time, rolled up in emotion, love and hurt—yes, you're right, this is the Arabian Sea. The song of its waters during high tide has entered through your seventh-floor window several times to reach your ears, but you haven't even come to know. That's fine, you didn't know this technique for selecting different sounds and analysing the levels. Now you do. Since you can't sleep, you might as well listen closely. Your friend and his wife are in Matheran for a day. You chose not to go with them. Poor things—they work so hard all week, let them have a day to themselves. Who asked you to be so generous and stay back in an unfamiliar flat? What does it sound like? You're right! The sea is calling you. That's how it is. The sea calls. It tells everyone to come and sit next to it. If only people could hear. The city is immersed in a haze of work, business and wealth. They will stand on the rocks by the sea and click away with their camera phones, but they cannot hear its music. Strange people.

Uh-oh! Just as I'd thought. I knew you would put on your T-shirt and jeans at once, get your walking shoes out of the rack, now you're checking in your pocket for the keys—I knew you'd go out in the middle of the night. I've done it too, many times. Just as well your friends aren't home. You take the sleeping lift to the ground floor of the tower. Just outside the gate is the three-way crossing. And across the road is the enormous gate leading into the garden. A green garden by the sea. Even ten years ago it was a dusty dumping ground. The richest people in the city come here for their morning and evening walks, which is why they have built a synthetic court, undulating lawns and a jogging track at enormous expense. Thousands of birds chirp on the countless gulmohar, almond and teak trees. And … then—as you walk you will see a swollen sheet of water stretching all the way from the horizon tumbling alongside you. But you've never come here in the morning. You're caked in the grime of the film studios by the time you return in the evening. Who feels like a walk after such a long day? You've registered the two scripts you brought. Now to bounce between studios, trying to get someone to buy them. Is that how you think it works? You don't even know the name of the woman who made the four hot rotis you gulped down—and you think you can write a film script? Tumhara naam kya hai, Basanti? So, you think this is how it works—J.K. Rowling, Ketan Mehta, Kiran Rao … very well, keep it up, we'll see.

The gate to the garden is locked. Naturally. No one is allowed to enter between nine p.m. and five a.m. Otherwise the antisocial types and the mafia dons will also turn up to gaze at the beauty of the sea. But is it really impossible to get in? There is a slight gap. You're not fat; this opening is enough for you. A watchman is sleeping near the gate, his arms behind his shoulder to prop his head up. Go ahead. The sea's calling out to you, after all.

A red gravel-strewn path winds its way through the trees and bushes towards the sea. Only a bit of the moonlight has been able to penetrate the thick canopy of leaves to reach the ground. But still, it's clear that tonight is not like other nights. Absent-mindedly following a curve in the path, you suddenly realise that the language of the earth has changed. The garden slopes upwards slightly, which was why the sea was out of sight. But now the bluish-white sea stretches out in front of you, all the way to the horizon; the music of its waves is in close proximity to your ears. The sound no longer seems to be a roar. The sea wants to clasp you ardently to its breast.

Yes, have you noticed that it's full moon—Purnima? It said Rakhi Purnima on the Marathi calendar in the kitchen—but then how would you have noticed—all this is Leela's responsibility.

Meanwhile you're standing on the seashore and gazing out to the south-west—what a scene! The full moon has shattered and dissolved into the towering waves. An urn of melting gold seems to have spread its tail out over the bluish-white sea. It's impossible to tear one's eyes away from it. You are looking at it too, entranced, when something suddenly stirs like a shadow at the edge of the water, where boulders have been resting since eternity. Who's there? Your hand has sneaked into your pocket without your knowledge. Although you don't have a pistol in there, you must do something in self-defence, mustn't you?

The figure sitting on the boulder is now moving slowly. No, not a man—a woman and, possibly, unarmed. Stepping out of her way, you stand at a distance. The moonlight is strong, there is nowhere to hide yourself, where can you possibly retreat? No, the woman has not noticed you, she is walking away with her head bowed, wiping her eyes with her churni. Oh, but this is our Leela! What's Leela doing here?

Now listen, the way you people clamp yourselves to your desks to write your screenplays is probably not the correct method. Do you want to know what Leela is doing here? After a hearty meal of her kofta and rotis you sat down to watch the Bengali channels on TV because you're homesick. But did you try to find out where Leela went, what she had for dinner or whether she even ate at all? So, you think the guest needn't bother about all this, those who should be bothered are in Matheran. But you're a writer—a storyteller; after all. You've just started writing screenplays for TV and cinema because it pays, but that should not change the way your mind works. Where is your compassionate, inclusive heart?

Then let me tell you, yes, I will, that Leela hasn't eaten yet. And with the darkness moving from midnight to dawn, the hour when she should have eaten has long passed. You can't have noticed the exhaustion that has been gathering on her pink, fair cheek and in the corners of her eyes since afternoon. But she did not neglect you. When one of the rotis was a little burnt, she made you another one to replace it—what about that! She hasn't eaten all day. It's Rakhi Purnima, you see. Raksha Bandhan. Ever since she moved to Mumbai, she has fixed a rakhi around her brother-in-law's wrist in the morning and given him a meal she has cooked herself. Her children, husband and sister eat too. That's why she cooked for you early in the morning and then took part of the day off—you remember now? From Mumbai by train to Delhi, and then another one to Aligarh, followed by five hours on a bus and then another hour on a bullock cart. That's how she gets to the village where her parents live. As a newly married woman she would weep constantly after leaving her home. She wasn't as capable then as she is now. Barely sixteen. She didn't even have an income. On the first Raksha Bandhan after her wedding, she had turned the house upside down, clamouring for her brother. That was when her newly married brother-in-law Surajkumar had said, all right, Leela, as long as you live in Mumbai, fix your rakhi on my wrist. That's how it has been ever since.

Having lived in several different slums, Leela and her husband finally settled in Asha Nagar. Her husband works at a building society nearby. Leela used to lock her two small children in their room and cook at people's houses. You're wincing. How awful. What if there was a fire …

'God would have looked after them,' Leela will tell you with a smile. 'How else are children of working mothers supposed to live?' By the grace of the same god of the poor, Leela's children are now six and eight. Leela herself is getting on for twenty-seven. She is practically the head of the family, bringing in nearly three-fourths of the family income. She has to work very hard, starting at five in the morning and going on till midnight. Both of them have to slave—cooking for the family, doing the dishes, washing the clothes, taking the children to school and coaching classes, and then their duties for their respective employers. Her husband has several bosses. But because he's a man, Leela's husband at least gets a cup of tea and a couple of handmade rotis when he gets home. I forgot to tell you his name: Vijay. Vijay Valmiki.

Do you know anything about people who have Valmiki as their surname? They are those whom the god Brahma created out of his own excreta and tasked with cleaning the garbage of the world. They are the mahitars—or, simply put, methars—who clean open latrines and drains. They are known by different names in different regions. Did I see you flinch? A methar's wife cooking your meals … aren't you a Marxist writer? You don't discriminate, surely. Do you believe in caste? Leela is so lovely and slim, with pink cheeks, large eyes, neat braids—can you imagine her hands reeking of slime? You cannot. Many of the gentlemen of the city assume Valmiki refers to the ancient poet, and some of them really don't bother. Some people, your friend, for example, cannot imagine this—just as you cannot. So it goes. Those who are not allowed to offer their guests a pitcher of water in their village, whose very presence near someone's house leads to the cooking being abandoned, can see how their descendants have melted into the metropolitan crowd, their caste identity wiped out. Here people are judged by their wealth or by their capacity for working hard. They slave till they drop. Leela and her husband have enrolled their children in English-medium schools, omitting their surnames. When they run to their parents in their monogrammed school uniforms, saying hi, Mummy, good morning, Daddy, all the effort seems worthwhile.

But this morning, how strange, Leela's brother-in-law Surajkumar did not turn up for the Rakhi ceremony. At nine-thirty he messaged her from his mobile to say he's busy, that he cannot come over now, that they'll meet in the evening. Vijay, too, went out in the morning. The man had turned very quiet of late, withdrawing into a shell, hardly speaking. He wasn't taking drugs or something, was he—Leela had wondered, fear welling up in her heart, and then forgotten the whole thing too as she got busy.

You know, in the course of this daily trip of yours to the film studios and offices in Andheri West from South Mumbai—which is affectionately referred to as SoBo—via Worli, and then the Sea Link to go further north, continuously along the expressway. You haven't passed any of the neighbourhoods spread across the north-western, eastern or far-eastern parts of the city. You haven't passed Govandi, Nalasopara, Mankhurd, Airoli, Malad, Kandivali—and the extremities of many other congested, rundown neighbourhoods teetering on the verge of death.

There are no sea-faces there, no decent roads, just some newly sprouted houses, along with uncovered drains and overcrowded slums—all these suburban areas occupy the fringes of the mainland. The outskirts of the islands have already been occupied by wealthy businessmen and the corporate upper-middle class. If you had visited those areas you'd have seen a multitude of matchbox one-room flats coming up in ugly, tall, rectangular multistoreyed buildings. Their beauty is matched by the technique of mixing thatching and water to construct these buildings.

In part out of their own desires, and in part at being moved by Leela's tears, Surajkumar and Vijay had made advance payments for two one-room flats in a neighbourhood of Nalasopara. One for each of them. Many other rootless people like them had also paid money to the same 'builder'. Vijay had borrowed from the building society he works in. His entire salary goes towards repaying the loan in instalments. Surajkumar had borrowed the same way—some of it from his employer, the rest from moneylenders. Once the flats are ready, they are to be given out on rent, augmenting their income. They don't want to live so far away.

Leela had said, 'This is how people in Mumbai get their own houses, bhaiya. Or else the water just slips through your fingers.'

The houses are being built—they have been visiting the site regularly to inspect the construction. The roof has been laid; the doors and windows are being installed. The keys to the flats will be handed over at Diwali. The builder took the final instalment at the beginning of this month. One lakh seventy-five thousand. Dirt cheap by Mumbai standards. Three years' wages for Vijay or Suraj.

Yes, they have had to toil for it, but the house is ready. Then why is Leela weeping by the sea at midnight? Their lives cannot have changed in a day, can they?

Actually, never mind an entire day—Leela's life has changed in the space of just five or ten minutes, at ten p.m.

I'm sure you don't know where Leela lives. All you know is that she comes in and leaves fifty times a day, her anklets ringing quietly. How can you get to know a person's address in just eight days, when you don't even know her name? When going out the front door, have you ever noticed the other small closed door nearby? You haven't, right? That's where Leela lives. A single room, ten feet by twelve feet. A tiny compartment carved out of the main areas of the flat—the servant's quarter. People like Leela and Vijay can lay down their lives, their honour, everything, for a space such as this in South Mumbai. Because so long as they have somewhere to live, they can acquire everything else—the wealthiest people live here, the most affluent of executives. The Leelas and Vijays will perform any physical labour for them, do any kind of work imaginable.

So, Vijay did not return to this compartment today. Suraj did. Drunk. Fortunately, the children were not there. Suraj's wife—Leela's elder sister—took them with her this morning. Sabita has no children of her own, so she brings her sister's children over on holidays. It relieves the load on Leela, gives her a few moments to relax.

Suraj heaped abuse on the missing Vijay. In Leela's presence. No Rakhi ceremony. The special meal lay uneaten. Leela's heart was bursting with tears. But even as Suraj slapped her, she wondered where her man had disappeared. He hadn't left for good, had he? And before her rose the image of the row of one-room flats in Nalasopara she saw earlier this month. The whitewash had seemed perfunctory. She had told Vijay surreptitiously that they must put one more coat of paint before they took possession.

Hearing the bad news from his neighbours, Suraj had raced off to Nalasopara. Was it just a rumour? The Nagarpalika authorities had pasted notices on the walls of the building three days ago. They didn't know what the notices said. At ten this morning, the road to the building complex was blocked off by huge municipality payloaders, dumpers, trucks and police vans. Like Suraj, another two dozen screaming and protesting people had stood watching their shiny new building being razed to the ground.

Where was the builder? Was he in town? Where was the absconding Suman Shah? Suraj had discovered that their builder—many other builders too—seeks out specific plots of land in Nalasopara, Mankhurd and similar areas to construct such buildings. They take advances from buyers—the buildings are even seen to be nearing completion. Then the owners of the land arrive to demolish the structures. Part of the payments made to the builder goes to these owners. The builder keeps the rest. It's a ring. Like the ring of work that Suraj and Vijay are involved in. This one also whirls in silence by daylight, with the intention of selling dreams of their own homes to the poor. The fools are taken in. Living in their ten foot by twelve foot rooms, they forget who they are, where they're from, how far they can progress.

What's that? Are you seriously asking why they didn't conduct a search to check whether the land did belong to the builder? Forget it—don't be taken in by the cheap printed shirts and sunglasses—do you think these Vijays and Surajs are even educated? Their village schoolmaster had long ago abused them for their caste and told them that the battle of literacy was not theirs to fight. They can neither read the notices nor understand legal documents. They have never tried reading a newspaper. How will they know who actually owns the plot of land? And besides, they have always assumed that builders and the government are one and the same. They never imagined one of them breaking buildings constructed by the other.

I see your jaws tightening. Excellent. You're furious, aren't you? Very good. The writer in you is emerging now. The revolutionary. But why not go to the police? Why not file an FIR? The fraud amounts to crores of rupees. No, sir—maybe they don't read the papers, but you do, don't you? It's true that TV has become national and global these days. It no longer broadcasts news about these localities. Didn't you read about the sweeper's daughter who passed her exams and became an engineer? She was molested—by goons. Her mother and brother went to the police station. They were thrashed after their clothes were torn off. The brother was framed in a case of theft. And why not—the goons were part of the councillor's team, and goons own the police. The girl eventually hanged herself to escape. A news item on page ten. An affectionate 'Naughty man!' from the party high command to the councillor.

They may not read the papers, but Suraj, Vijay and their friends are smarter than you are, you see; they know the police inside out. So they will never go to the police. What's been lost is the backbreaking labour put in by a hundred families for three years. Let's say three times hundred—three hundred years of human work has been eliminated from the calculations. So what? Eternity remains.

Tchah! Just think of the harm I've done whining to you about an age-old story which will never be turned into a screenplay. Where's the moon now? Where's the golden tail fanning out over the water? The sea is retreating slowly in the darkness after the setting of the moon. The high tide has ended. Low tide is beginning. The sea knows that even its continuous roaring needs a temporary break.

You've taken off your shoes, but you're lying in bed now without taking off your T-shirt and jeans. Your arms are folded beneath your head. Can't you sleep yet? You will, you will sleep now. It's getting to be light outside. How long can a man stay awake? But now you have discovered yet another level of sound, admit it. The muffled sound of Leela weeping, beneath the roaring of the waves. You'll have to separate it from the rest and listen to it carefully. I know you can. You're a writer, after all.

You fell asleep without realising it. Now the blue sea and beach adjoining the garden are sparkling in the sunlight. This is how each new day arrives, obliterating the memory of the night. Just as well. That's what man lives for.

There, Leela has unlocked the door and come in. She has bathed and dressed in her pink churidar-kameez to camouflage her reddened, swollen eyes. With a lovely smile she is telling you, 'Wake up, sahib, I'll bring you your tea.'

THE DECEIVERS

The river Betwa had flooded, its turbid water overflowing both its banks. A river whose ribs were visible in winter had turned so very powerful now! The water level was rising irresistibly. The roots of the trees on the other bank had been visible even a short while earlier. Now the trees were submerged up to their ankles. There was indeed a long bridge spanning the river, referred to hereabouts as a rapta—but the saffron water was flowing furiously at least a man's height higher than the bridge.

Ravikant stared at the water for a long time. The monsoon wind induced a shiver, but Ravi's clenched fists were perspiring. Fear trickled down his spine. At the district headquarters they had told him that the water level was slightly higher than the bridge, and that it would go down at night. You can cross the river on the tractor to reach Bharatpura. Or else there was always the ferryboat. Fortunately, the tractor driver had all but slapped them, saying, 'You idiots!' and the ferry boatman had already run away the previous day—which was why the polling party for Bharatpura had to wait at the dharamshala.

Not that the tractor would have dared to cross the river in any circumstances. But what if the boatman had decided to make the journey in a moment of recklessness? By now five corpses would have floated up to the surface of the saffron water, with a crowd of people on this bank to identify the corpses.

It was a late Monday afternoon in September. The lowering sky was ready to burst. It had rained incessantly for the past eleven or twelve days. It paused at times, but only to lash the mountains and forests twice as hard. Those who had been lining the bank all this while, watching the water rush past and joking about the habits of the Betwa, were now headed homeward with annoyed faces. Stale water dripped off their umbrellas on one another. Across the river, a narrow trail wound its way through the forest, as though it had just emerged from the water and shaken itself dry. That was the way to Bharatpura. Darkness would soon claim the faint, solitary sign of their destination.

Ravi couldn't spot even a faint orange glow in the west. The dilapidated balconies of Jahangir Mahal sprayed blue and yellow parrots across the overcast sky and then took them back again. Jahangir Mahal on this side of the river, Sheesh Mahal on the other, the memorials to the Bundela along the bank, and the ruined, desolate, gaping entrance to the camel stables all stood in silence, the imminent darkness wrapped around their heads. For two and a half centuries they had been witness to the swelling of the muddy waters in June and July. The water had tinged their foundation walls with a thick coating of moss, sometimes dislodging a marble slab or two in sport and taking them away.

A disheartened Ravi was surrounded by the other four when he returned to the dharamshala. As though fresh news had been brewing in just one hour, which Ravikant had bought like a packet of hot jalebis at the riverside. Ravikant was the head of the polling party at Bharatpura—the presiding officer. He was a junior engineer in the irrigation department. Three of the other four were primary- and middle-school teachers. And the fifth was the peon Buaram.

Five strangers from different departments and schools in the southern part of the district had been put together like a salad and sent to the north. No team would have two people from the same place. And they would have to go to unfamiliar villages. The names and addresses of the members of hundreds of other polling parties like Ravi's had been swirling helplessly in the computer. Using a mysterious incantation, their destination had been pulled out from the bowels of the machine last evening—Bharatpura. Unbreakable impartiality and unshakeable detachment—only with these could the polling party conduct the ideal form of voting. How could democracy exist without these? No one would know even a couple of days in advance, and there would be no familiar faces—or else the electoral process would acquire the black mark of bias.

'Did we have to get Bharatpura?' Misra, the middle-school teacher, was tearing up slices of dry bread to eat, carefully, so that the food didn't come into contact with anyone else. Misra had had bad luck, or else why would his party have to have people from the Ahirwar and Kushwaha communities? He couldn't possibly accept food or drink from people of these castes. Of course, the primary-school teacher Mangal Ahirwar and the peon Buaram were so apprehensive already that Misra needn't have been so careful.

Did they have to draw Bharatpura? Was there anyone in this district who didn't know that Bharatpura in the rains and exile on a desert island were synonymous? Bharatpura was a solitary habitation, like an eye between the rivers Betrawati, aka Betwa, in the north and Jamni in the south. In winter buses ran in both directions, since the rivers were buried under sand then. From the end of June, buses and tractors ran with care, only after gauging the height of the water over the bridge.

This time the monsoon had arrived late, like a maniac, and there had been continuous rain since the middle of September. Several of the villages were waist-deep in water and the roads were damaged badly—but none of this would lead to the aam chunao being postponed. The dates for the aam chunao or the Lok Sabha elections had been announced three months earlier—only after eminent scientists, engineers and meteorologists had submitted their reports had the dates been finalised. They couldn't possibly have known about a dark corner of the country named Bharatpura.

Thursday was voting day. There were two days to go, but the polling party was out of breath already. Imagine travelling such a long distance just for the sake of democracy. They had reached the district headquarters at dawn on Sunday, after journeying about four hours by bus. After a quick meal, they had had to queue up under the fabric canopy outside the high school to collect the voting equipment. It had been raining then too. Wet and exhausted, they had waited to get their equipment. Rows of labelled buses were lined up on the main road. Each of them would deposit six or seven polling parties at the district headquarters or the panchayat office. Buaram had the ballot box on his shoulder; Ahirwar, a bundle; Misra had the voters' list tied up with rope and dangling from his hand. They had to carry their own suitcase and bedding too.

It was evening by the time they reached the sub-divisional headquarters in the north. What a road, my god! Gigantic potholes everywhere, thanks to the constant movement of ramshackle tractors. Here a truck had pitched face-first into a thorn-apple bush, there a bridge was about to collapse. The constant droning of crickets was deafening even in daylight when driving through continuous forests of arjun, asan and siris trees. Millions of rupees were poured into the roads every year, with the contractors siphoning away most of it. Many of them didn't even go through the formality of actually appointing labourers—the whole thing existed only on paper. So, by the time Ravikant Singh's team arrived at the sub-divisional headquarters with aching spines and shoulders, there was a large moon in the sky—it was the night before full moon—with scattered clouds around it.

From here the tractor would go as far as the banks of the Betwa—and then, if the water was low enough, it would take them all the way to Bharatpura.

The tractor carried them like a load of bricks or stones, rattling them to their bones. It was the agricultural season, but the government had confiscated the tractor on the grounds of elections. The farmer's curse rained over the polling party. They didn't even have the chance to nap, for they might slip off in that case. They felt as though they were clinging to the body of a gigantic reptile.

It was past midnight. Not a soul out in the countryside. A couple of greedy leopards were prowling about cowsheds. The monsoon wind blew in their faces. Misra had covered his ears but couldn't stave off an attack of sneezes. Another man named Lakshminarayan Pathera got off once and retched his guts out on the slopes by the road. Ravikant, the presiding officer, smelt trouble. How relieved he'd be when the entire polling party reached the polling station.

The river had dispensed evil advice to them that night. The clouds had not been as thick as in the evening—the flawless moon radiated beams like notes of classical music. In the moonlight, the flowing water of the river had looked like millions of mermaids. The bridge had been submerged, the opposite bank had looked dim and uncertain, and yet Ravikant had said, 'Let's cross over.' The others had looked at him, overwhelmed, as though powerless to contradict him. But at least the tractor driver Roshan was a simple man, who had shown no sign of being taken in by the black magic of the water. So, dubbing them idiots and lunatics in his hoarse voice, he had dropped the polling party at the Jain dharamshala near the river. The elections were two days away. What if the water level did not go down tomorrow? What would they do? The polling party would have to wait for the water to recede until the returning officer ordered them to return.

On Monday evening Ravikant headed for the market. He wanted to make a phone call. They had no phone at home. If he phoned the neighbours, they would fetch his wife. His son had been diagnosed with jaundice. A lively boy of fourteen, now lying in bed like a limp rag. Two jaundice patients had died at the government hospital just a few days ago. Ravi ached with anxiety constantly. On reading the letter summoning him to election duty, his wife Sujata had said, 'Every year there will be elections, and you will have to abandon your family and go off somewhere risking your life—the last time you were in bed for three days when they beat you up. I wonder where they're despatching you this time.'

The skirmish, when he had been injured by an attack with sticks, reminded him of Patel. There had been trouble at their booth last year. Brandishing guns, spears and sticks, hoodlums from the Opposition party had snatched the ballot papers out of their hands and started stamping them. Since it was the Opposition, the police arrived in droves. Indiscriminate use of their batons. And since they were members of the Central Force, they couldn't tell the polling party apart from the public. Ravi was hit on the shoulder, and Patel, on the head. Patel fell unconscious. He was treated at the district headquarters. But no one had said anything about a scan at the time. About six months later Patel developed a terrible pain in the head, losing vision in one eye. His speech began to slur. He had returned from the hospital in Vellore about a month ago, half his body paralysed. Patel was fast becoming one of the rejects.

Would Sujata be able to cope in case Raju got worse? She probably would, for she was a strong woman, but it was very difficult to get a hospital bed. He had informed the neighbours, even his boss Manohar Tripathi. Ravikant tried continuously but simply couldn't get through on the phone. Lights were going on in the small market town shops. Tourists thronged here in winter to see the royal palaces and the river—the town had no life at this time of the year. But at least the place had electricity—once they reached Bharatpura, they would have to depend on the lantern and water from wells.

'My name is Muneshwar. I'm the village barber, responsible for all of you. I have instructions from the panchayat.'

The polling party stared in surprise at the man who had just said this in a hoarse voice. It was ten-thirty in the morning on Wednesday. They had reached Bharatpura about an hour ago, mud-water stains all the way up to their chests. Their bodies hadn't stopped trembling from the cold, and they were still wracked by thirst. They wanted to bathe and change their clothes, but where was the water? The walls of the primary school were mouldering with damp, and had huge cracks in them. The sky was visible through the tile roof. The floor was littered with slabs of cement, stones, leaves and twigs—no one had even bothered to sweep them away. Four scared goats were clustered together in one corner of the veranda, their dung scattered around them. A bundle of hay lay on one side—probably fodder for the goats.

This was the polling station. This was where people of Bharatpura would vote the next day—provided the school building survived another day and night, provided it didn't collapse and bury the polling party.

'No tube wells or wells hereabouts, Muneshwarji? We haven't even washed our hands yet,' Ravikant managed to rasp with great effort.

Muneshwar was a man of spectacular appearance. He was nearly six feet tall, dressed in a khaki shirt and floppy blue pyjamas ending well above his ankles. But both the shirt and pyjamas were tattered and stained. His hair stood on end, his face was unshaven, his nails were long. It was obvious that the village didn't have another barber.

'I'll get you water. There are buckets too. It'll take a little time. A cur fell into the well and is rotting in it—you can't use that water. Have a hot cup of tea meanwhile ...'

Several young boys and girls were peeping out from behind Muneshwar. Some of them were bare-bodied, while others were dressed in wrinkled, outsized shirts, which they had pulled out of their pots and pans and put on in honour of the polling party. Taking the kettle from a boy, Muneshwar poured the tea into glasses, four fingers of his left hand, complete with their long nails, sinking into the hot tea. Ravi averted his gaze, and Misra felt his stomach churn, but they finished their tea in desperation. Muneshwar was the straw they had to cling to in this dark, dilapidated settlement of Bharatpura.

The battle for votes had intensified in the capital. Film stars were presenting their song-and-dance routines in support of different political parties. Old scams and scandals were being dusted out in the open. The roads and markets were abuzz. No newspapers would write about how the polling party of Bharatpura had risked their lives to cross the river. Someone from the police station had visited the dharamshala late on Monday night. The polling party was about to wrap themselves in sheets and go to bed after a meal of boiled rice. The mosquitoes were the size of twenty-five-paise coins, ready to bite whenever they found the small patch of bare skin. The Betwa was flowing with a roar in the darkness. The sound of the water had settled inside the polling party's heads since dawn. When the chowkidar from the police station started calling for them, Ravikant had had to put on his pants and go out. Most annoying. Whenever anything happened, it was always the presiding officer they called.

Despite the static on the wireless set, they could extricate the information that the water level would drop by Tuesday night. The polling party should cross the rapta and set off for Bharatpura early Wednesday morning. The voting was on Thursday. Polling would take place across the constituency, because all the polling parties had somehow managed to reach their destination. Now the office of the superintendent of police was relaying a message from the returning officer for Bharatpura—the polling party, cowards that they were, must set off on Wednesday morning …

This time the tractor driver Roshan did not hurl invectives at them. There was no rain on Wednesday morning, but the sky was overcast. Monday and Tuesday had seen torrential rain over several hours. And yet the river had indeed subsided, although the extent of its saffron surface was just as wide, as was the upheaval of its currents. But the level had dropped, for the backbone of the cement bridge was now clearly visible through the water. The water was deeper in mid-river, but a tractor would pass.

'How did the water drop so much in one night, overseer sahib?' asked Mangal Ahirwar anxiously before climbing on the tractor. Misra muttered the names of the gods. The overseer, meaning Ravikant, said nothing, although he knew that the flow of blood in this southbound river was controlled from the capital. That's where the huge Pandu dam was located. When it threatened to burst under the force of the water, the sluice gates were opened to let the water flow southward. When the gates were closed again, the force of the water went down. Faced by the relentless rain, the government had had no option but to open the sluice gates, which was why the Betwa had flooded near Bharatpura. Maybe they had closed the gates last night.

His face like stone, Roshan stared ahead as he drove the tractor through the saffron water stretching to the horizon on either side. The polling party was soaked by the continuously splashing water; none of them said a word, their teeth clenched. 'He Ram, He Janki,' Misra mumbled tearfully, whereupon Roshan stopped him with a snarl. 'Shut up, if the tractor capsizes, all of us will be swept away ...'

The vehicle lumbered along very slowly with its cargo of equipment and human beings. If they went any faster, the water would draw them down into its depths, but if they went slower, the vehicle would not make progress. Ravikant felt that the road was unending, that they would never reach Bharatpura—a big bulb kept going on and off in his head. What if they died before reaching!

As they drank the tea in which Muneshwar the barber had dipped his nails, the polling party dimly felt that they were indeed alive. Their hearts were returning slowly to their rightful places. Misra's stock of bread and flattened rice had run out. He could barely croak. Probably out of sheer survival instinct, he agreed to eat whatever Muneshwar the barber would cook for them. On the condition, however, that the water from the well with the dead dog couldn't be used. Mangal Ahirwar was groaning with fever ... lying on a scrap of tarpaulin in a corner. His head and throat had both started aching even before they had completed the crossing. 'They haven't provided medicines this time,' said Buaram frantically.

He was right! Ravikant rummaged through the equipment they had put in the corner of the room. The ballot box, bundles of ballot paper, glue, shellac, seals, stamp pads, inkpots ... all of these lay there like faded toys—insignificant, insensate ammunition in the apocalyptic war of the election. On other occasions there was usually a packet of medicines—they had probably forgotten it this time. It normally contained chloroquine, pills for fever and upset stomachs, and a purple tincture for cuts and wounds.

Ravikant tested Mangal's fever with his palm. He had a few fever pills of his own, one of which he would give Ahirwar.

Belying their fears, the voting was completed without any rigging. Not a sign of booth-capturing. Many of Bharatpura's inhabitants were besieged by malaria, moving about wrapped in blankets even in the daytime. No one attacked them with sticks, either. For the reedy home guard and the amulet-flashing forest guard were the only security personnel at the polling booth. They did have a stick each, but trying to use them would only have meant injuring each other.

On Thursday morning, the polling party was ready with the room cleaned up, the table set up and the ballot box placed behind a curtain of jute. Muneshwar had done most of the work single-handed, personally sweeping the floor clean of the hay and dung. But where were the voters? They came in ones and twos as the day progressed, peeping in, without the courage to step inside. The presiding officer called them in to make them vote. Two polling agents had appeared with glum expressions, spending some time sitting on a sheet of jute. One of them ran away, supposedly stepping out for a few minutes, and did not reappear. Later in the day, the women appeared in a group—after they had finished their cooking and fed their men. Clogs clattering, saris rustling, they nudged one another and giggled, embarrassed at the sight of unfamiliar men.

One of them simply couldn't find the slit in the ballot box. Ravikant had no choice but to peep in behind the jute curtain. They were too shy even to hold their fingers out for the ink mark signifying that they had voted, balling their fists instead. The behaviour of two old women made Ravi suspicious—they were stealing away furtively. 'Where are you going, Buri-ma?' he called out to them. Caught, they smiled with their toothless gums—they had wrapped the ballot paper in their saris.

'Have you stamped them? Come and put the paper in the box.'

The old women looked at each other. If they put them in the box, what would they show the people at home? They had woken up at dawn and walked such a long way to vote!

The weather turned ominous on Thursday afternoon. The wind picked up speed. Muneshwar had brought word from the ferry boatman that it had been raining torrentially in the capital since the day before yesterday. The only radio set in Bharatpura, which was at the grocery, rumbled out the same news. The polling party had sealed the ballot box after the voting had ended and tied it up in sheets. They had packed their belongings. Darkness fell. With it, the sound of the water became louder. The Betwa had been rising since the afternoon, its turbid water hissing and growling as it flowed over the rapta.

The polling had been completed peacefully in the entire region. In Bharatpura too. But now Ravikant and his team were pincered. How were they to leave?

Five human beings sat within the cracked, mouldy walls. Mangal Ahirwar's condition had worsened—he wasn't even groaning anymore. The villagers had returned home after voting. Muneshwar the barber's responsibilities had been discharged too, but he had not left. Wandering about in his dirty, unwashed shirt and pyjamas, he was like a messenger of defeat—the water was flowing two feet higher than the rapta, three feet, two and a half feet …

They didn't speak to one another anymore, even eating in silence when Muneshwar brought them rice and daal. Ravikant tried desperately to picture his son's face. If he suddenly took a turn for the worse, would Sujata be able to cope? He no longer felt an ache in his heart, only a blunt, lifeless void. They had released water from the Pandu dam in the capital. They would save themselves first, obviously. That's why the Betwa was flooding again in the south. The elections were over. What did the government care for marooned polling parties? Their work had been taken care of.

Friday, Saturday, Sunday … the days passed like a moving black wall. Why on earth had he asked Roshan to go back with the tractor on Wednesday afternoon? Ravikant rued his decision. He would have felt more confident had Roshan been here. Actually, they had assumed that the water level had dropped for good, that it wouldn't rise again.

On Monday morning, serving them tea in which he had dipped his nails, Muneshwar said, 'I see no sign of the water receding. The boat is gone, the boatman is hiding. The rascals have cheated you, getting you into Bharatpura by lowering the water flow into the Betwa … and now that the work is done, you're of no value to them … one doesn't need to pass examinations to understand all this.'

The counting was scheduled at a much later date this time. There was a fortnight to go. The government would definitely evacuate them if they needed to open the ballot box. They would send a helicopter if need be. For now, there was no hurry. The heart of democracy was beating in the sealed and bound green box. They were merely the bearers.

Ravikant knew. But still something rang loudly in his head when he heard Muneshwar say the word 'cheated'. His eyes smarted. He wished he could say … you're wrong. The government will definitely send a rescue team for us, just wait and watch. A helicopter will come …

No one came. Morning made way for afternoon. All of creation was covered by a saffron river and the sound of its water.

ARCHAEOMELANCHOLY AND THE WATER

A plump, solemn cloud appeared, showering torrential rain on the Sunabera plateau. It was impossible hereabouts to determine who the father of this cloud was—a depression or a cyclone. There wasn't even electricity here, never mind television. A transistor radio rumbled once in a blue moon in the hands of someone passing in the dark like an aged tiger—fading in a while. The newspapers came very late. No one had the slightest inclination to read such stale news printed in the local language on poor newsprint. Sudhamoy Nanda had constructed a neat barrier around himself. Thin and stooping a little, Sudhamoy discovered that his thick glasses were bringing distant things closer these days, while taking nearby objects further away. For a long time, his new bifocals had made him totter around like a child learning to walk. But that was a long time ago. The horizontal break in the lens had fragmented Sudhamoy's line of vision into two. He was no longer inclined to recognise people quickly—nor could anyone touch him the first time they met. Shaking the water off his wings like the cloud, he lived a silent, intense existence.

Sudhamoy Nanda was standing on the mound of Chandanmahal now. The earth was filled with a wondrous yellow light after the rain. Crickets buzzed in the wild bushes around, although it was daylight. The late afternoon was so quiet that it appeared ready to blend into the evening on tiptoes without telling anyone.

Moo … Shambaru Paharia's calf lowed before fastening its mouth on the teats of the golden silence. There was a view here of what lay below. The mound was not particularly high. But still Kanchan Sagar was visible in the distance—the water covered by a multitude of red lotuses. The mound was surrounded by a mixed jungle of weeds, wild jujubes, arjun, gum and kino. A little further to the north-east, a few families that had abandoned Ankatoli had built shanties for themselves. Beyond that was the fenced camp office that Sudhamoy worked in. To the right of the new shanties was a narrow walking trail. The original Ankatoli slums lay along this trail.

Nobody lived there anymore—they had all left. Before abandoning the mud hovels to move to the new slums, they had uprooted and taken away as much of the bamboo sticks, the straw, the tiles and the doors and windows as possible. Two years of sun and rain after this had all but destroyed the houses. Only the deserted veranda of Lakshman Singh Samanta's house with the long latticed railing was visible from this mound.

Would it rain tonight? This wasn't the time for rain actually. It was the end of May. The monsoon had not even begun its journey inland yet—it was still flexing its limbs in its mother's womb somewhere in the southern seas. Even the slightest drizzle would make old Picharu's team lethargic about working tomorrow. It was unbearably hot today. Their efforts to work were sporadic.

This particular mound at Chandanmahal was higher than the surrounding ones—and larger too. About fifteen years ago, King Dani's hillock by the river Jank was excavated to discover a Shiva temple with Kosala architecture. It had created a minor sensation among experts. Excavations at Chandanmahal had started soon afterwards. Layers of earth had been removed with great care to reveal terracotta bricks, fragments of urns and a square pit about twenty feet deep. Perhaps this used to be the treasure chest of the habitation. Sudhamoy Nanda believed something like a watchtower stood on this mound, for only from this height was the entire valley visible. There used to be a secret chamber beneath—as was obvious to anyone—and further digging might reveal a trapdoor with steps leading lower, much lower.

The Jank was not visible from this spot. A dense green line of forest stood halfway between the Kanchan Sagar and the river. If the eye could look beyond this line, the river might have come into view. It was strewn with rocks and more rocks. Two streams of water warbled between them.

The river had straggled down with aimless steps from an empty height above the Sunabera plateau. Many, many centuries ago. No one had questioned its behaviour for a long time thereafter. People in this area had died in the drought of 1943. Unofficial sources had revealed tales of human and animal skeletons lying by the road during the famine of 1966. Buffeted successively by drought and aridity, people suddenly told themselves—why not put manacles on this tyrannical river? Someone said, the left canal can irrigate eleven hundred and twenty hectares, and the right canal, twenty-two hundred and five hectares. Preparations for a survey got underway. The earth was still being excavated in this valley. Cadaverous labourers excavated the land, taking leave for Chaitra Parba, Nuakhai, Karma and such occasions. Terracotta bricks, foundations of rows of buildings, the sanctum sanctorum of temples and dried stepwells were emerging from the depths of an area of almost five square miles. At that point, everyone had assumed that the work could continue at this same pace—there was no hurry, after all. Sudhamoy's mentor Afzal Asad would say, Harappa and Mohenjo-daro were excavated over several years. This wasn't child's play—not a matter of digging a lake, where you got hold of a hundred labourers and let their spades loose. This was an art. The spade and the shovel and the crowbar were its paintbrush, and the illiterate rural labourer, its sculptor. Their loving touch coaxed the sleeping world of the past to shed its garments of dust under the surface of the earth and rise slowly to the surface.

But the time allocated to the archaeological formations on the Sunabera plateau turned out to be limited. The survey of the land for the dam had barely ended when the complicated processes of land acquisition got underway. After which, typically, the price of the land in the nearby village began to shoot skyward. It was bound to, since the people of villages like Ankatoli, Ramnagura and Telibhasha would now have to abandon their homes and look for new places to settle down in.

The news had spread like wildfire. The water was on its way, the water. The water was coming. The river would be dammed. Six nearby villages would be submerged in the huge lake that the dam would create. Even Kanchan Sagar, its surface teeming with the lotuses that they had used all this time to decorate the entrance to the village. The grazing grounds near the old habitations would be submerged. Yes, the pillars and the other artefacts of the ancient civilisation that had been dug up would all be submerged too. Not that the villagers were bothered. All this was a personal matter for their 'gold-seeker babu', Sudhamoy Nanda.

Along with the bricks, fragments of clay pots and figurines, small and slender gold discs—possibly used as coins—stones like topaz and beads had also been unearthed. All of them had been gathered carefully, wrapped in cotton wool and stored in glass bottles. The aged Picharu Binda had helped Sudhamoy considerably. He must have been over seventy—though he looked even older—bent over and unable to walk properly. When he sat down, his chin brushed his knees. People in this area loved and obeyed him. Unless he lifted his lean arm and gave the signal, none of them would join the work. Besides this, Picharu watched intently when the specimens were arranged in groups at the camp office, with squares being marked off on the floor with lime solution. As he watched, Picharu became drowsy at times. Saliva dribbled from his mouth, wetting his knees. Sudhamoy had explained matters of history to him as best as he could, but his own muddled thinking had led the old man to believe that all these excavations in the earth were actually a case of digging for gold. Sudhamoy had arrived from the city in his canvas shoes and shirt and trousers to search for gold so that he could take it back with him.

Poverty, enteric disease and cerebral fever had leeched these hills and forests since way back when. People started leaving the villages in search of work elsewhere well before the onset of the monsoon. The rate for daily labour was higher in the neighbouring Raigarh area. Meanwhile, there was a swarm of moneylenders at the back door. In September the rice would ripen, but it would run out by the advent of winter, after which they would have to resort to ragi porridge, boiled mahua fruit and mango kernels …

People had started leaving their homes for years altogether now amidst the uproar over the impending flood. Ankatoli was the first to be deserted. It was dead in the centre of the giant lake that would be created. Then the people of Ramnagura, Telibhasha and Chilkalchua began to move out gradually in search of fresh pastures and forests and livelihoods.

These six or seven villages were mostly occupied by Gonds, Bhunjias and Paharias. The Paharias used to be blacksmiths once, but now they were bamboo artisans. The Bhunjias were divided into two classes—the Chindas were cultivators, while the Chakrias either indulged in slash-and-burn cultivation on the mountain slopes or hunted. The Gonds were milkmen. All the large herds of cows hereabouts belonged to them. Sudhamoy could not understand the Loriya dialect of Chhattisgarh at first, but now he could converse passably in it. He even exchanged a joke or two with the labourers sometimes, although they normally maintained sad and solemn expressions in civilised society.

Sudhamoy had been standing on the Chandanmahal mound for a long time, watching dusk descend on the earth. The sun was a huge orange ball beneath the clouds. Just before the world sank into darkness, he would pick his way carefully back to camp with the help of a torch. Maniram would have cooked him a dhundhul curry and rice. When Sudhamoy would stretch himself out on his camp cot after his meal, dressed in a lungi and a vest, the cries of the nightbirds and flashes of the haphazard, wistful scent of oleanders would rush in and try to lull his tired body into sleep. A profusion of oleanders had bloomed on both sides of the narrow walking trail that led to Ankatoli—the locals called it kurei. So many things here that made Sudhamoy melancholy. He just couldn't cope with them anymore.

This period before the descent of dusk was a very strange time. A transcendental earth, beyond the reach of the senses, took advantage of the darkness to spread its wings. The Nishada and Kosala kingdoms had risen such a long time ago. The Narmada's birthplace was Amarkantaka—according to Cunningham, the area between Amarkantaka in the north and the source of the Mahanadi in the south, and the Wainganga valley in the west and the river Jank in the east was the Mahakosala kingdom. On Ashoka's thirteenth pillar, this area was called the Atavik Pradesh. The Mauryas had never succeeded in conquering it. If the latitude and longitude of the place described in the Mahabharata as Giriprastha, the wondrous capital of the kingdom of Nishada, were to be calculated, it would turn out to be located somewhere near Ankatoli. Hiuen Tsang had travelled to the Mahakosala kingdom—Watters had written—sometime between 630 and 645 CE. The capital of the kingdom was here in the Jank valley. Maybe Hiuen Tsang had even walked along this very unpaved trail, past the Ankatoli that no longer existed now, to the river. Had the women of the town peeped out of their windows for a glimpse? Did the children follow him, drawn by his strange garments, chewing on blades of grass? Not even the forefathers of these trees here were present at the time. The ancestors of these birds had not been born—but other trees, other birds, other species and even the river must have been there, witness to Hiuen Tsang's presence.

When darkness was about to fall and the constant calls of the birds quietened down, a mist of sadness like a fine rain rose from the heart of the earth to envelop Sudhamoy. The now-silenced cries of those who lived here twelve hundred years ago in those underground rows of small earthen houses, of those who gossiped around the sunken rock-lined draw-well on such evenings, of the invisible figures of the town commissioner, the temple priest, the treasury guard, the sage and the women and the children—all these drew random lines across the earth. The water was approaching; the spillway was at work round the clock, in three shifts. At night the work proceeded under floodlights. The dam was slowly nearing completion, about to brim over with water. An electric current spread across the earth at the sound of the armed footsteps of the currents. Everything would be submerged, all of this—the capital of the Mahakosala kingdom brought painstakingly out from beneath the surface of the earth—would drown. Much, much later, when a fat black rohu jumped out of the water in the afternoon sun, no one would know whether an underground temptress's laughter had slid across its gills. But all that would happen much later. Right now, a stricken question that had rent the fields and the forests apart weighed down Sudhamoy's heart like a rock … Sudhamoy will save us, won't he? He will take us away before the water reaches, won't he?

Nonsense, how could he! He could barely keep his own body and soul together. Sudhamoy alone knew how hard-up he was. The money never came on time from headquarters. He almost always received his salary after the fifteenth of the month. There could have been serious trouble over payments to the labourers, but since there was no union and only the aged Picharu, he managed. Those who could work really hard had all left for other villages, other lands—only the rejects had stayed back. The pace of work was slow here. The spades and shovels and pickaxes were wielded with long gaps in between, and Sudhamoy had to make do with these reedy men close to old age. Eight years ago, when he had just arrived, he used to run from pillar to post for funds. Racking his brains, he had prepared a project report with colourful covers in pink, blue and yellow. The reports had been sent to Delhi and Mumbai and even to Paris, but no one had responded. All these years later, everyone knew that no one would respond. The only response was to the people's hunger and the panting thirst of the parched land—the water was on its way. Like a transparent upper garment, the water would cover all these stifled underground groans.

Sudhamoy had visited the old and derelict area of Ankatoli a few days ago. There was no sign of rain that day and the late afternoon sun was blazing down. Quite unexpectedly, he had run into rather an odd man with a prematurely aged face, salt-and-pepper hair, a gamchha slung over his shoulder, dressed in a blue shirt and a dhoti. A bunch of amulets and roots hung around his neck.

He had emerged slowly from a completely dilapidated building. What was he doing there? Was it a ghost by daylight? Sudhamoy had been startled. He had said his name was Sahadeva, a Gond. Sudhamoy should have guessed, because several cows—white, black, brown—had been roaming around the deserted, abandoned area.

'What are you doing here?'

Sahadeva had been mumbling to himself in the Loriya dialect, his moist and pensive eyes wandering all over Ankatoli. Such a strange tongue. Sudhamoy had never heard anything like it in his life. 'Main iga chhor deh. Huzoor ihar mor ghar rahis, ihar mor purkha baapmaanke bhitamati rahis, naowa gaane rehbaar mor man ni laagthe …' He had continued in this vein.

Sahadeva had left his home here to buy land and build a house in a different village, but this was his ancestral home. However, his cattle didn't care for the new home—they kept tugging at him every afternoon to go back. His cows came away to graze on the grounds adjacent to Ankatoli, practically dragging him along. Once here, he walked around his own abandoned house. A dead, dry arjun tree stood across the unpaved road running in front of his house. The village deity used to be worshipped beneath this tree. The villagers had taken the idol away before leaving. Gradually the tree died too, as though it had lost the will to live in this deserted neighbourhood.

Gold-seeker babu, Sahadeva had called out to Sudhamoy from the back, the government told us to leave our village in a hurry, everyone made a lot of noise about how we would be submerged by the water—but where's the water? They could have let us stay in our own homes a few years more. What harm would it have done? Sudhamoy had not been prepared for this question. He held his handkerchief against his nose, pretending to cover it from the dust raised by the hooves of Sahadeva's cows. What could he have said? Ankatoli had been split apart—the houses separated from the farmland. The limited compensation had lost the battle against the rising land prices. Fathers and sons were separated. Uncles and nephews no longer met in the villages they had moved into. When the project trucks lined up on the day of departure to collect and transport their belongings, a wave of tears had washed over Ankatoli. Mothers and daughters had wept with their arms round one another, while able-bodied men had rolled on the ground in grief at the prospect of leaving their homes. Sudhamoy's world had blurred behind his glasses that day, but what had he achieved? The work on the dam had not progressed on schedule. Iron and cement had become costlier. The contractor had taken all the money due to him, while the engineers had presented reports of time overruns to the auditors—Sahadeva and the rest of them could easily have stayed on in their ancestral homes for a couple of years more. Would the people who had forced them out be asked for explanations?

Sudhamoy had no answers on this wistful evening. Just as he had not found the answers to any of his own questions either. Was there anyone whom he could ask: Could my life have been different? At the precise spot at the centre of the Chandanmahal mound where the deep excavation of the treasure chamber was underway lay a dead, uprooted, colourless kino tree. Creases of agony were etched into its bark, its crooked branches reaching out towards the sky in a silent fossil scream. He had had a meagre research grant at the time, a few published papers too—but no ground beneath his feet, no job. Why would Ruma have left him otherwise? After Ruma had left, Pratima had appeared, following the unchangeable laws of nature—but what had he given her, for that matter? Their frail son had been born even before eight months in the womb, torn out of Pratima's body prematurely in a bid to save her life. He hadn't managed to stand up till six or talk before seven. Now, at twelve, he could walk holding on to the wall, dribbling from the mouth constantly. He would picture Ruma's face every time he made love to his wife. Sudhamoy could not push that radiance away despite all his efforts. Was that why the sapling didn't bloom? Who had the answer? A constant routine of prayers and rituals had made Pratima age prematurely—the huge dab of vermilion on her forehead smudged, several black and red threads tied around her wrist. Why did Sudhamoy have to be posted here in this remote jungle? Why did he not have a godfather? Reams of applications, and even a court case at the end—Sudhamoy had left no stone unturned. Had Pratima's bangles dwindled gradually into those red and black threads? Still, he had not been able to escape the labyrinth. Sudhamoy's future was destined to be drowned, just like the archaeological rocks or Ankatoli.

Pratima had not wanted to let him go this time. How long could he extend his holidays—two days or three at most. He had to come away eventually. Gathering his clothes from the rack, Sudhamoy was packing his suitcase. There was a power cut—in the dim light, the giant smudge on Pratima's forehead came very close to him, searching for something in his eyes with a sad gaze.

'You're not keeping any of that gold with yourself, are you? Please don't—it isn't good gold, it's been lying next to people's bones underground. Given our condition, greed could make it worse, I'm very scared.'

The people here called him the gold-seeker babu. It was both true and untrue. A lot of gold foil and pieces of gold had been excavated at the beginning. The group leader or the mate would quietly pocket them. The aged Picharu had not been all that old then—he used to visit the mound regularly. The old man had often smiled guiltily at Sudhamoy while tucking the loot away in the garment fastened around his waist. Skeletal figures from a famine-ridden land—Sudhamoy could not bring himself to pull them up. Just the other day four young labourers—practically boys—had died when the earth collapsed on them while they were digging a tunnel to collect illegal topazes. The trader from another land disappeared instantly. The boys' parents could not even wail in grief. It wasn't as though Sudhamoy didn't have a few such pieces of gold foil wrapped in secret cotton wool in his trunk. The new constable at the police outpost had often clapped him on the shoulder playfully, asking for a look. Sudhamoy had evaded the request grimly. The foils were unusual—round, not uniform, with an unfamiliar script etched on them. The indistinct face of a woman was visible on one of them, and the mystery of how the ethereal smile on her face was inscribed on the foil had not yet been unravelled …

The days were passing one by one now, summer giving way to the monsoon, the monsoon to autumn and winter. All sorts of wonders were emerging as successive layers of the earth were peeled away. The more the chain of steel and concrete tightened around the waist of the river, the surer Sudhamoy grew that he would not be able to restore the bangles on Pratima's wrists that had wasted away and been lost. But still he glanced at the pieces of gold foil before he went to bed every night, smelling them. He could not bring himself to throw them away. Sudhamoy knew that the water would rush in unexpectedly one midnight, making his cot shake, setting the trunk loose on its currents, and draw Sudhamoy into its noisy, pulsating torrents; he would then begin his life with the men, women and children who lay underground—much, much later, when a huge black rohu leapt out of the water, no one would come to know that Ankatoli's gold-seeker babu had still not found the ground beneath his feet.

THE POET'S HOUSE

The neem tree cast its shadow directly in front of the poet's house. In this shade had grown a berry and a tamarind tree. The neem was old. There used to be several fruit trees here earlier—mango, guava and so on. The saline water had killed them. Young poets from Calcutta had often eaten the mangoes and guavas from these trees. If they managed to grow, the berry and tamarind trees would have fruits too. It was to be hoped that their lifespans would last that long. Half-reclining in his bed, the poet gazed out through the small window with bamboo strips as bars. The eyes have memories too, just like the mind. The mango tree no longer existed, but he could clearly see its gnarled trunk and the wood ants climbing up and down its bark. The eyes had not changed their habit just because the tree no longer existed.

Thick tea made with sugarcane gur and ginger in a tall glass. Just like a decoction. It got rid of all the stiffness in the body. Cleared his throat. Phlegm gathered these days in the upper half of the respiratory tract in the morning. Made his breath heavy. And yet, it wasn't as cold as it should have been at this time of the year. He was getting older, that was all, his age announcing itself through his body.

The poet's house was in the northernmost corner of the island. Two rivers surrounded the island on both sides. The one on the right was named Gomar and the one on the left, Vidya. A bank of silt had risen in the Vidya, close to the far bank. On the near bank, the strong currents of the river at high tide kept eroding the base of the embankment. The river went on shifting its course in this way. The Gomar was shifting in the same way as the Vidya. Waking up late at night, he could often hear the cries of birds that preferred the darkness, and the splashing of the water during high tide.

The embankment seemed to stretch across the earth for thousands of miles. Ever since the zamindars had secured their rights to the land here, they had been getting ryots to put up embankments and repair them every year to ensure that the river could not flood their habitations. The free supply of physical labour had kept life going in this river-girdled existence. All this was the responsibility of the independent government now. One look at the embankment was enough to see how well the responsibility had been discharged. Uneven patchwork, the bricks showing through. Portions of the embankment kept collapsing in storm and rain, and subservient contractors stuffed stones and bricks into place again. No one was concerned with the future. Having ceded land continuously to the embankment, the farmers had no extra land now. Those who had lost their homes in Cyclone Aila now lived under polythene shelters next to the embankment. They spent sleepless nights, listening to the high tide in the darkness. With the currents threatening, sleep was impossible.

The sound of the water no longer evoked a romantic longing in the poet's mind as it used to when he was young. Instead, a choking melancholy assailed his sleep. At first sight, though, he seemed the perfect householder—there was a kitchen garden, plants, cattle and poultry, and some farmland surrounding the couple's home. The poet had no conspicuous fear of losing any of this. But actually, the continued existence of all that was visible and present now was extremely uncertain. However, this sense of uncertainty had not yet dissolved itself completely in the poet's consciousness. Just like oil and water don't mix, it floated as a separate layer, making the poet uncomfortable. In his own small bed at night, he tried to listen to the distinct sounds of his wife and daughter breathing; it seemed … there's no one there … only complete silence! That was when fear showed itself—am I all alone in the darkness then? Is the breath of the water unwilling to tolerate any other spark of life? Getting out of bed quickly, he lit a match and brought the lamp closer. A little later, he could be seen walking around the house with the lamp in his hand. In the impenetrable darkness, the slightest touch of light on the poet's eyelids woke her up. Sleepily she said, what's the matter, go to bed, Mithu and I are fine, we're sleeping …

Aila's stormy winds and the fury of the water had turned the placid life in the village upside down. The earth and the water and the people in this area were ever-changing—the poet had known this before he moved here. Here a sandbank would appear in the middle of the river; there a perennial river might dry up. Elsewhere, erosion took a river all the way into a human habitation. Landless outsiders had appeared on the newly claimed land to set up home, while families who had lost their homes to the river were moving elsewhere in search of security. The land degraded faster in the forest areas adjacent to Bangladesh. Much of it was swallowed by the water constantly flicking its tongue. After a long time, roots of sundari trees began to be found beneath family homes—as though the sunken earth had slipped through a crack while asleep and been buried under the top layer of civilisation. Although land degradation was not as widespread in this part of Bengal, it was a routine affair for the portion beneath the embankment to be worn away constantly, with fissures developing. Using a set of carnivorous jaws, teeth and tongue, the water—stretching to the horizon—seemed to constantly gnaw and eat away all that was protected inside people's homes. Such was its fury that it didn't even leave behind the earth it had taken bites of, the waves carrying the chunks elsewhere, where new islands rose from the river.

Storms, floods and earthquakes visit human beings three or four times every century to find out how things are with them. As far as memory could recall, there had been a powerful cyclone twenty years ago too. But it had nothing in common with Aila. So unexpected, so overwhelming, cunning, swift and murderous. Even now, a year and a half later, when the poet thought of those days in May, he relived the crisis of not being able to reconcile the uncertain with life.

'Purno, are you home, Purno?'

Brajaraj appeared outside the house to hail him as soon as it was morning.

It took a while to respond—sheer laziness. He didn't feel in fine fettle. By then Brajaraj had called out twice more already.

'Is Purno still asleep, Boudi?'

The poet's wife understood Brajaraj's restlessness very well. He wouldn't even accept a cup of tea at this hour. His dearest wish was to get the poet out of bed and into the streets. The early morning air was very clean, although the scent of salt percolated into the very earth here. The river and the greenery shone in the golden morning—a walk at this time lifted the spirits. Ever since his youth, Brajaraj had worked in the soil department of an old voluntary organisation in the village. He was also interested in discovering medicinal plants. For a year or so now, Brajaraj had nurtured the desire to spread the light of this knowledge amongst the tender young boys and girls who went to school. So, he had started making up short rhymes about these plants and passing them on to schoolchildren. Apparently this would enable them to identify plants right from childhood and learn of their properties. But Brajaraj's handwriting was not very good, and there were many students, which was why he had leaflets printed at the local press, paying for them himself. But he always showed the poems to the poet before sending them off to the press—the end-rhymes, rhythms, alliteration, etc., had to be perfect.

Even the budding poet Brajaraj had not been spared Aila's fury. No, his house hadn't collapsed—nor had his farmland been seriously damaged. The danger came from a different source. Brajaraj was a member of the all-party committee set up to prepare a village-wise report of the damage inflicted by Aila. He had almost been beaten up in the course of this work. Apparently there was no need to actually check the extent of damage. But unless they could inflate the extent of the losses as much as possible and add as many people to the list as they could, their village would not receive enough money. The other areas would take it away. Brajaraj had not been keen on signing this fictitious list. 'All of you can sign if you want,' he had said, 'but I won't be a part of this fraud.'

'You think you're the upholder of the truth,' the other members of the committee had jeered at him and threatened to beat him up. 'Get out,' they said, 'we'll sign for you.' How humiliating. Almost to avenge this humiliation, the Centre didn't approve even one-tenth of the compensation claimed. Whatever money did come ran out even before it could be distributed. The destitute villages remained with the festering wounds from the storm, the death and the destruction.

On this beautiful winter morning, though, Brajaraj certainly had no unhappy scars in his mind. But still the poet was reminded of the all-party committee when he saw him. All kinds of plants and vines lay along their way, many of which the poet was familiar with. But Brajaraj was testing his knowledge laughingly, asking him various questions. The latest set of poems had given the poet the impression that Brajaraj had made the methods of alleviation more complicated than the illness—but explaining this to him was very difficult.

Example: Brajaraj had written in his poem that applying the juice of cotton leaves with salt cured ringworm. Excellent. But if this led to complications, papaya sap would have to be applied, and the pain would have to be borne. Why? What use was the papaya sap? Again, applying lemon juice with basil leaf juice also cured ringworm in a few days. In the same way, nettle rash had to be treated with the sap of telakucha leaves every morning. This was the simple method. And yet Brajaraj had written in the course of the same poem that applying a mixture of fifteen grams each of khoi and neem leaves, five grams of white sandalwood paste and haritan, and of grated seashells, would cure nettle rash in a fortnight. How much grated seashell? Brajaraj hadn't mentioned. Just as he had not stated earlier how long it would take to cure nettle rash with telakucha leaf sap. Clearly, important information had been left out for the sake of the rhythm and rhyme. It would probably have been better to write it all in prose form. But if he said this over and over again, Brajaraj would be hurt. He would conclude that the poet was trying to tell him that writing poetry wasn't easy. Who would provide the medicinal plants to cure this wound? Therefore, the poet did not offer too much of his opinion these days, sticking to praise instead.

In this locality at the extremity of the island, the houses were not far apart. The conversations and laughter, as well as the bellowing of the cattle, from one house could be heard in the next one. Space was hard to come by. The poet's paddy fields were behind his house. It was less than an acre of land, but he couldn't manage it himself anymore. Thanks to age and the problems of sharecropping, he had to take the help of farmhands. Had the land been in front of the house, even this paltry source of income would have been wiped out by now. The Vidya ran in front of the house. During Aila it had broken through the embankment, flooding the house and the paddy field. About a kilometre's length of embankment was destroyed. Once the salt water had subsided, the fear of the killer of October loomed large. Fresh embankments were put up hastily. Unpaid labour by poverty-stricken people. As a result, the embankment was not broad enough, the bricks not set securely, the lumps of earth not levelled, the path uneven. Newcomers would stumble at every step. Locals became familiar with the humps and potholes while a road was being made. They could navigate it even with their eyes closed. But even earth was hard to come by. The upper layer of soil from the farms adjacent to the embankment had been used for the repairs. Call it an embankment—meant to stop the river from eroding the land—or call it a path. The salt water had infiltrated so far that the plots next to the embankment were all ponds now.

The path ran beyond the berry and tamarind trees, skirting Jiten Mridha's house, and passing between two ponds. The poet was walking with his eyes on the ground. A little distracted. Brajaraj was behind him. In the still water of the ponds was the fresh reflection of an aged drumstick tree with a twisted hip. The blue sky and the patterns created by the clouds were all visible in the water. Was a different world being created underground—to be occupied by those who had been evicted at the goading of the river? The poet turned to look at Brajaraj. Loud sobs floated in on the wind. Brajaraj had his ears pricked in an attempt to listen.

The villagers spoke to passers-by without a reason here. People also enquired after one another without any reason.

Sunando Misra was Jiten Mridha's neighbour. Snatches of the sound of someone crying could be heard. Misra's mother had passed away at the crack of dawn today. As a neighbour the poet should have visited him. And yet he felt no urge. Brajaraj was a social creature through and through. He had been to Sunando Misra's house early in the morning to express his sorrow. After which he had gone to fetch the poet.

'Ginni-ma was suffering a great deal,' said Brajaraj. 'Just as well she's gone. She's been released.'

The poet was walking in silence. Absently. When they reached the embankment they discovered that the low tide had given way to the high tide. Like the back of an enormous grey turtle, the silt bank adjacent to the distant bank of the river was being submerged, very, very slowly.

Saluting death first thing in the morning. An arduous task. The poet hadn't been able to do it. He would go later. Even if those taking the body away had left by then, he would leave a fistful of flowers by the bed.

A column of young women trudged along the embankment in front of them. It wasn't wide enough to walk two abreast. So, the conversations were with the person in front or behind. All of them were women from Pubpara, here for a last glimpse of the lady who had died. Even though they didn't mention anyone by name, the context was clear.

'Last night too she asked about the almanac date apparently ...'

'That's right, she used to say she didn't want to die after the full moon ...'

'She told her son where she put all the money ...'

'And do you know what she said?' said Buma. '"I won't harm any of you in any way, but I will be nearby, make sure Khoka gets enough to eat. And don't beat him ... I can't take it."'

The poet realised that the woman was quoting Sunando Misra's mother's last words, using her own dialect—just like the tongues of Jessore and Khulna, the oral dialects of Midnapore were also in use in these areas.

Sunando Misra's grandfather had come here from Midnapore to inspect the newly acquired land. After Hamilton had set up his settlement, the local zamindars used to build embankments around each of the newly sprung islands. Or rather, they had the embankments built. Using local farmers and labourers as unpaid workers. That was where a group of people had taken land on lease to start farming and living. Those were very hard days. The islands were constantly destroyed and rebuilt in sport between the sea and the river and the earth. There were jungles of sundari, garan and hetal trees. Salt water. Mud. Snakes, tigers, leeches, fever, accidental death. A farmer's life would end before he could carve a farm out of the jungle for himself and get his first harvest. The next generation would work even harder to make the land even more fertile. They gathered wood from the forest to build sturdy homes. Setting up a new habitation was backbreaking labour. How would today's young men, who whiled their time away with games of cards and carrom, understand any of this?

The zamindar's orders, the zamindar's whims. There were no remnants of the tears that had been shed or the blood that had flowed in the first years of land acquisition. Squads of private soldiers armed with sticks and spears would keep bankrupt labourers from the Mal area of Bihar, Midnapore and East Bengal continuously on the run, like herds of animals. They were not allowed to clear out the jungle anywhere and settle down—they were forced to keep moving, converting even more dangerous areas, deep within the forest, into land habitable by humans. Some of them did manage to secure leases on the acquired land and got involved in cultivation, but the others, unable to put down roots anywhere, kept moving and working themselves to the bone till the day they died.

The Misras did not settle here all that far back, however. Less than a hundred years ago, which meant that the zamindar was a recent addition to his tribe. But he was just as whimsical and unpredictable. Resting beneath the trees after lunch, Misra and some other men had thrown away their bidi stubs before crossing the river later in the afternoon and setting off for Midnapore. He didn't even know that the sparks from the bidis had started a fire that had burnt down a large section of the forest. The zamindar sent for Misra through his relations. Fearing punishment for starting a fire, he returned apprehensively from Midnapore and meekly confessed his crime. 'Yes, we were the ones who threw our bidi stubs into the distance, we didn't realise the dry leaves and grass would catch fire so quickly, and that it would spread so far.'

The zamindar said, 'Your punishment is farming the land you've burnt. I will provide the seed, but the labour and ploughing are your responsibility.'

Hardly a harsh sentence. The delighted Misras arrived to settle on their new land. All this was such a long time ago. Why the delight, wondered the poet. Sunando Misra had told the story. The third generation of the original settlers. The story now sounded like a fairy tale of altruism. All that land given to the family just because the jungle had been burnt down by a fire caused by bidi stubs.

Actually, it was a case of buying the blood, sweat and tears of the landless without any payment, along with their gratitude. The new cultivator was responsible for all the physical labour and the animals needed for ploughing. There was no market price for labour. The story made it appear as though the land was given free of cost. In fact, the zamindar purchased his taxes at the throwaway price of a few seeds. Looked at this way, it was a story of the oppression of the homeless. This was how the poet knitted his thoughts together as he walked along.

The women who had been lagging behind had gathered pace, overtaking them in ragged lines. They were probably in a hurry. Loads of unfinished chores at home. The lines of alta on their cracked heels were fading.

At the sight of their feet Brajaraj muttered:

'Mango sap
in bottle and cap
If you find your heels are cracked
Use it for a cure, that's a fact.'

'On your right, Purno, take a look. This is thumbai. And there, that's a moss rose. You know what it's good for? You can use it for snakebite. Another name for thumbai is dronapushpi.'

'Really? Should I plant some near the house?'

The soil expert in Brajaraj emerged at once. He was no longer a faithful devotee of the poet's.

'Oh no, that won't work. There are several differences in the soil. Medicinal plants that grow near ponds will not necessarily grow next to your house.'

The postmaster, Ashok Dhara, was wheeling his cycle towards them. The latest version of the embankment was so skeletal and uneven that it took real courage to ride a cycle on it. The postmaster was not willing to take such a great risk.

'Going to Calcutta today, Purno-babu?'

'Not today, tomorrow. But only if they come to fetch me. I can't walk all that way on the bridge after reaching Canning from Gadkhali. Even if I don't take my umbrella, I do have to take my bag ...'

'Let me tell you something—they'll start measuring the land for the new embankment today. I heard at the BDO's office. I suggest you stay here for the next two days. The people making the measurements will need you.'

'Is that so? Then should I stay? Not that I had anything particularly important to do. Just an invitation to give a speech somewhere. What speech could I have given—I would just have read some of my poems.'

Behind him, the soil expert Brajaraj protested vehemently. 'Go, go if you want to. You must make our village famous. I'm here for the measurements, Boudi too. And anyway, all my life I've seen them measuring the land, but nothing comes of it. I keep hearing that a new embankment will come up … just keep hearing.'

The poet felt a trifle mournful on hearing all this. Every time the river broke through the embankment, the farmer lost his land so that a new embankment could be built. For he had to give up his land and move his farm elsewhere. How else was the embankment to be built? But no one gave the farmer any compensation for his land. Those who lost their houses for the sake of the embankment had to find somewhere else to live, without any arrangements for rehabilitation. People had faced up to extreme damage after Aila—they had watched their friends and family die of thirst, the cyclone had killed birds and beasts, the salt water had ruined the crops in the field and the potable water. Now if they had to give up their land again for a new embankment—for a larger embankment …

Ashok Dhara shook his head. 'No, Brajaraj, you don't get it. This isn't the same as what's been happening all your life. After Aila they're serious about this. The measurements in

Chhotomollakhali and Satjelia are done, the government is even buying the land for rehabilitation at one go this time …'

'I'd better stay back in that case.' The poet was aware that even the warmth of the sun had not melted his gloom. His feet stopped in the courtyard even before he could enter his home. How beautiful, he thought. And yet these were his own riches.

A sweet, spirited female voice was uttering the poet's own words, written long ago—

'This cloudless afternoon in late autumn—
The air silent, the jungle dark, sodden earth below,
Sometimes singing birds and chirping insects
The leaf on the tree lustrous with grace
A drop of kindness from the sun playing on it
But how long can the silence last?
The narrow trail is thorny, fresh tiger and deer footprints
Alone, uncaring on this forest path
But how long—how long can I stay unmoved?'

The poet's elder daughter rose from her seat when she saw her father. The boy of seven with her was eating a meal of milk, muri and gur with great concentration. Large drops of milk dripped on the floor.

'I'm glad you're back, Baba. I came early in case you went out. Which poem should I read in school—this one or "The storm lasted till yesterday" …'

'The storm didn't last till yesterday, Ma,' the poet said with a smile. 'This one, I think.'

Tranquil now, the poet washed his hands and feet.

His elder daughter had married someone in the same village. She had two children. She managed her household and taught in the primary school. She recited beautifully. Although almost all his poems were written from a male standpoint, the poet felt that they acquired a different dimension when his elder daughter recited them. Tomorrow was the foundation day of their school. The daughter would read the father's poetry.

Shanta's was a sensitive mind, but she was also obstinate and became emotional easily. During Aila, the poet and his daughter had come close to cutting off all relations. How horrible! Even death would have been preferable. The poet loved both his daughters deeply, embracing them with all his consciousness and compassion.

On the day that Aila struck, it had been drizzling from the morning. In the first half of the night, the sound of the rain mingled with sleep. There was a summer depression in the Bay of Bengal. Stormy winds. At about nine in the morning, the floods came, unexpectedly. No one had predicted such force. The embankment was swept away wherever it was weak. Where the embankment did not break, the water simply jumped over it, submerging homes, farmland, ponds and tube wells in an instant—where there had been ponds adjacent to the destroyed embankment, as was the case quite often in these parts, an entire river now flowed. Humans, cattle and poultry all drowned to death in thousands. Fortunately, it had not happened at night—people were awake—or else the thousands could have turned into tens of thousands. The horror didn't end despite the number of deaths. Instead, an even more terrible period of thirst, hunger and disease began. The salt water had got in everywhere. It receded routinely every day and then returned at high tide through the gaps in the embankment. Day after day this continued—for a month in some places, a month and a half in others. Three hundred thousand, four hundred thousand people were dying of thirst. Corpses of human beings and carcasses of animals and birds and snakes rotted everywhere. The water smelt foul—had the river rotted away completely?

The poet still remembered—and trembled deep within himself at the memory—how the floor and the sheets would be black with flies. A stench everywhere, mosquitoes, no water, no electricity. In the dark without electric lights, fetid salt water overflowed the yard during high tide, entering the house. Its height inside the room was still evident in the form of a stain on the wall. Two or three bookshelves had stood waist-deep in water, the books on the lower racks completely ruined, the letters obliterated. Later, the poet had tried desperately to resuscitate the books by laying them out in the October sun—but to no effect. Perhaps out of unbearable hurt, the books rotted. Several of his poetry notebooks were still lying damp, the writing smudged. Picking them up made the memory of the agony come alive.

Shanta's husband's home was on higher land, and the water had not entered it during Aila. But the entire village was submerged. She had to wade through the water continuously, sometimes with food in tiffin carriers, sometimes with potable water in bottles. Leave this house and move in with me, she kept entreating her parents. Their younger daughter had been at a relative's house in Calcutta when Aila hit. Word was sent to her to stay there. The poet categorically refused to abandon his house. And yet he couldn't provide a clear reason for his refusal either. How could his wife leave him behind? So both of them remained, unbearably imprisoned. The tide alternated between high and low every six hours. Sitting in the darkness and listening to the gurgling entry of the water and to its receding footsteps could turn any sane individual mad. Their daughter coaxed and cajoled every day, weeping; their son-in-law begged them; his parents sent handwritten notes. Eventually their indignant daughter stopped visiting them. She could not understand why her father wasn't ready to move in with them even for a few days. What she didn't know was that this house was the poet's ark during the apocalypse. Abandoning it meant a voyage towards complete uncertainty. Also, the negation of a lifelong existence. He had built this home on this land at twenty-two, freshly arrived from Midnapore. His new bride had stood beneath the mango tree in the yard of this same house. The poet had not had the heart to take away the heartbeat of the home when it was besieged by the darkness and the flood.

As a young man, Purno had arrived here in the Sundarbans not to settle on newly acquired land, but because he was attracted by the people and nature. The ancestral house and family farmland were in Midnapore—but he didn't have any roots there in that sense. Visiting some distant relatives, he grew fond of all the new images—the reflection of the afternoon in the village tank. The fence of herbs around the house, the pacing of deer in the extensive wooded area, the invisible presence of tigers, the moonlight flooding the sky above the confluence of the Vidya and the Gomar, the agreeable local people—these were the reasons he had come. The house that the poet had built with his own hands was a poem celebrating the fact that he had lowered anchor in this village. How could he abandon his home even in a crisis?

The new bride of those years was in a plain sari now, her hair uncombed this morning, slicing vegetables and putting the fish in the pot to cook. Perhaps she had water droplets on her fingers, making the oil on them crackle. Their younger daughter would eat, of course, and she was hoping to distract her grandson into eating too.

The poet let his body rest in the swing made of rope that hung in the space between the two rooms. It was very comfortable to lie in, reading a book or the newspaper. For writing he had his traditional small bed, on which he sat to write. It wasn't possible to write while lying down, after all. A home wasn't built overnight. It had to grow bit by bit. In terms of visual appeal, however, the poet's house was not particularly captivating. It was practically hexagonal in shape, although it had been rectangular to begin with—a single room and a veranda. Later, considering the size of the plot, another room had been added. The veranda had acquired a wall and become the kitchen. A curtain of palm leaves kept the sun out. The roof on the right had been made afresh with tin and wood, but the one on the left was still a fragile patchwork of palm leaves, bamboo and straw. Aila had pushed the people of the Sundarbans fifty years back overnight. Bereft of crops, food and cattle and poultry, they had abandoned all their embellishments, their music, their festivals—everything. Even in the poet's house, the whitewash had not been renewed since last year. Still the women had drawn leaves and flowers on the walls with vermilion and chalk, and the large oleanders seemed to have struck dancing poses. The poet had not drawn them, but the women in the family had. They made the house look so much more beautiful. The poet looked at them in contentment.

'The fever-bee vibrates on my body a million times
All of me is a thirst when I step into your sunshine'

His elder daughter had left behind the poetry book of thirty-two pages printed in a small press in Midnapore. The book was more than forty years old. The covers had come apart, the binding was loose. The poems were raring to fly into the air any time.

From Midnapore to the Sundarbans. The challenging period of going beyond a playful life to setting up a home and starting a family. He had ploughed the fields, sowed the seeds, harvested and cleaned and stored his crop—all with his own hands.

In his dhoti and shirt, he had read his poems on Calcutta's well-lit stages. Despite the dirt of the Sundarbans in his nails, the poet had never had to resort to tricks to bring the worlds together. Just like the tiger lurks in silence inside the jungle, concealing its black and yellow lightning, the poet's personal, solitary existence began the moment he crossed the Vidya on the ferry.

'The fury of the river breached the embankment …
The salt water gushed into the paddy fields …
When the low tide came the repairs began.
A violent storm struck yesterday—its teeth and nails
Left deep scratches all over the body of the village …
The agony of the pain is still in their eyes.'

A major initiative had begun at the embankment now. The riverbed had risen considerably—not slightly, as earlier. Now a big embankment would be built after all the measurements were made. Dhara had said as much this morning. But the poet had heard it too from people in the irrigation department. The embankment would be moved more than three hundred feet away from the current one, and it would be much higher too. Everyone was anxious about the land that would have to be released. Even in this village, those who had houses or land near the river had had to move twice or thrice. All that land had been swallowed by the embankment or the river. No one anywhere had got any compensation—nor in this village. They were hearing that the government had bought land elsewhere to rehabilitate those who would have to move once again in order to ensure a clearance of three hundred feet. No easy business, purchasing so much land.

The poet felt drowsy in his swing. He thought it wouldn't be right to go to sleep here. The land revenue people would be here for the measurements, along with the irrigation department. When they arrived, they would see a man sleeping comfortably in the swing, his own tattered book of poems on his chest. To those who had to do all their work in the sun, this would be an annoying sight rather than a pleasant one.

Sitting on his bed, the poet ran his eyes over the notebook covered with Brajaraj's script. What on earth had Brajaraj done? He had written that bleeding could be treated with grated tender garan tree leaves, grated rice in the juice of grass shoots and pounded berry leaves; burns could be treated by roasting the bark of banyan trees and mixing it with coconut oil—so much bloodletting, so many fires in the hearts of the people of the Sundarbans, the garan forests, the verdant plains, the grandeur of the berries and the banyan trees—all of these would be destroyed.

He had dropped off with his head on the pillow—by the time he awoke, the somnolent yellow late afternoon of

November had arrived. Doves and magpies sang all around the house. His elder daughter had left with her son in tow. Some of the child's toys were strewn on the floor. His younger daughter was probably out as well.

'May we have some water, Mashima?'

An unfamiliar voice was heard outside.

Three or four young men and one middle-aged man stood outside the window. Since it was afternoon, the sun was still strong. Winter hadn't arrived in full strength yet.

The men had beads of perspiration on their foreheads and the shirts on their backs were wet.

They were carrying measuring tapes and notebooks. 'What do you think?' asked the middle-aged man.

'Won't work, Dada.'

'Why not?'

'Three hundred feet from the embankment on the Vidya this side, three hundred feet from the embankment on the Gomar on the other side—and then the land for the embankment itself—how much room will that leave for the house?'

They were here to take the measurements. They couldn't see the poet lying on his bed inside the room. The government had purchased land for new colonies to be created for the houses that the embankment would swallow. The same team that was taking the measurements would have to draw up a list of the future inhabitants of those colonies.

Fifty years. The age of this family home. Not a particularly long period in the history of civilisation. The government team entrusted with taking the measurements stood outside, passing the death sentence on the poet's house, which the poet listened to from his bed. Sitting there, he could see the fence of herbs, the branches of dancing five-petalled oleanders on the wall, the cat sleeping by the clay oven in the kitchen. The announcement made by the team was now rushing into the poet's brain cells the way the salt water streamed in through cracks in the embankment—no, bleeding or burning must not be allowed now. This moment needed to be captured in poetry at once.

The strangers had asked for water. The poet's wife was organising things. They had a stock of cane gur round the year. She was pounding the chunks with a pestle and mortar to serve them on brass plates. She had got the bronze tumblers down too. They weren't used every day, being set aside for special occasions. So, she was washing them with care, using tamarind and ash. The tumblers must not stink when the guests drank water out of them. The homemaker's face radiated deep kindness and contentment. She did not know the outcome of the measurements.

Sitting on his bed, the poet tried to freeze this moment with his eyes, his head, all his nerves. Not much longer, possibly as early as next July, the rippling, restless water would flow here, and crocodiles would surface with a splash. Or ancient turtles and the moonlight would play on the crest of the waves, and famished tigers would swim across the river to attack people's homes. And yet the law blocked humans from entering the forest, which was why the hungry people had left the land, while innumerable women, children and old people sat in their houses with the doors locked against the night—those who could not go away.

The poet could see the dark July night—sitting here in daylight in his own house, which had been marked for death …

the berry and the tamarind trees in the courtyard had been submerged. Because the neem tree was taller, its head and its leafless branches jutted out of the water. Perhaps the fishing boat of khirish wood which used to be tied to the trunk of the black tree near the embankment would be floating near the poet's bedroom. Since the river would have obliterated the family home by then, a few worn pages from the book of poems, the letters on the sheets of the manuscript wiped out, would be moving further and further south with the ebbing tide, becoming one with the expanse of the ocean stretching to the horizon.

SAROJBALA

'Sarayu, ey Sarayu ...'

'Sarojbala ...'

Sitting with her back to the wall, Sarojbala was not exactly lost in thought. But it doesn't always register immediately when you're addressed by an unfamiliar name. Raghu, the cook, peeped in to tell her, 'Badhi-Ma is asking for you.'

Sarojbala jumped to her feet. That's right, it was long past seven-thirty. She had given the old lady her medicine at a quarter to seven.

'Coming, Badhi-Ma, I'll make your rotis now.'

'It's past seven-thirty, I've been calling you for ages, you never pay attention ...'

'It won't take long, Badhi-Ma, I'm making your rotis right now.'

Won't take long was just something she said. Of course, it would. Badhi-Ma wouldn't eat unless the food was steaming hot. Her meal consisted of two courses, and it took her some time to chew each mouthful. And yet, everything had to be equally hot. It had confused Sarojbala at first, her brain almost vaporising—but now, after nearly a month and a half, things had fallen into place. The first course was a bowl of milk and a roti. The milk had to be piping hot, but not the roti, for hot rotis were too hard to eat, apparently. The roti had to be torn into smaller pieces and slipped into the milk, but not before a large spoonful of sugar had been stirred in. Sarojbala warmed the daal along with the milk on the gas stove, using adjacent burners. But the gas had to be turned low, otherwise the daal would get too hot. It took about five to seven minutes for her to eat the milk-and-roti, after which the daal and rice had to be served. Unlike the rotis, the rice could not be cool. It had to be steaming hot—the daal too. Which meant that the pressure cooker with the rice in it had to be put on the stove as soon as the milk was taken off, so that steam was rising from both the daal and the rice by the time they were served. She had to take each of the bowls carefully from the kitchen to the dining table. Small wooden coasters were laid out on the table to prevent the glass from cracking in the distant future. Heat was not good for glass. The bowls had to be placed on the coasters. Something might turn cold in the process of being brought in from the kitchen. The point was not whether it really had turned cold. Even if she were to touch the bowl to show Badhi-Ma, here, see how hot it is, or, it's still steaming, the old woman might not accept it. Her principal objective in life was to ensure that no one could deceive her about the temperature of her food. So Sarojbala had to go back to the kitchen with the steaming bowl …

When she had a few moments to herself, Sarojbala sometimes thought about her own meals. She sat in a circle on the floor with her daughter, son-in-law and grandchildren to eat. It was more economical to eat together. There was less wastage too. They had no refrigerator, so in the summer there was always the fear of the leftovers rotting. Serving herself a small portion of rotis and vegetables, Saroj checked whether any of the others had extra food on their plate or were going to waste what they had. Especially her grandchildren—both her daughter and she ate what was left over on their plates. Gradually her own plate filled with rejected vegetables, rice mixed with curry but not eaten, bits of potatoes, fish bones. A hot meal? Saroj didn't remember the last time she had had one. Hunger cared for neither warm food nor cold—and besides, who would pay for the fuel needed to warm the food again and again?

Her daughter was under a lot of pressure. She had taken on a second job at Badhi-Ma's, along with her regular one. She got a headache every evening. Her shoulders and back ached, too. Before going to bed, a whole pile of dishes had to be washed outside the door of the communal bathroom they shared with other families. 'I have to, the children have to be brought up properly, they must be educated … What do we have to sell besides physical labour?'

They lived in the service quarters adjacent to the flat in which her daughter worked. A room and a shared bathroom. Even this tiny space commanded a rent of ten thousand rupees a month, in addition to an initial payment of a couple of hundred thousand. There was no lack of people in Mumbai ready to pay these amounts for a room in a slum. They must not let go of this room, no matter that the plaster was flaking off the walls and the floor was worn out. The children went to school nearby, their private tutor was close by too, and the sea was next door, with a beautiful park next to it …

Her daughter couldn't afford to lose this room, which is why she worked so hard at the Bakshi household. And she had given her mother the job of looking after Badhi-Ma—she simply couldn't afford to turn this opportunity down. They needed the money. There was no question of handing over this job to anyone else as long as they were alive.

'We need money, Ma, lots of money.' Sarojbala's daughter whispered so sibilantly, her eyes round like saucers, that she actually found it funny. Her son and daughter-in-law were struggling on a starvation diet in a Delhi slum. Living with them was as hard as leaving them was. Delhi winters chilled you to the bone, while the summers boiled your innards—but still, she had grown used to it over all these years. Her son's factory had been locked out for ten months, and the four thousand rupees that used to come in every month had vanished. Contractors had dug up all of Delhi in preparation for the Commonwealth Games. Saroj's son had been working as a labourer for one of them. But some sort of investigation had stalled the contractors' payments and, with them, her son's wages. That was when he and his wife told her, 'We'll get by somehow, but you'd better go live with your daughter. Even if all you do is look after the children, it'll give her some respite.'

Such a gap between imagination and reality! This was like entering and exiting the tiger's cage every day.

Badhi-Ma was done with her dinner. Sarojbala would now have to hold her chair steady as the old woman rose to her feet. Then she would have to lead her away gingerly to wash her hands, change her clothes and put on her nightdress, pour her a glass of fresh water, and arrange the blankets and quilts near her feet. None of this was heavy labour. Her daughter used to do all this earlier but now she only did the dishes. It wouldn't be safe for Sarojbala to have anything to do with water in the evenings at this age—even if not like in Delhi, there was a wind from the north and the west in the evening in this flat, and it was quite chilly after sunset.

Did they hire people here at such large salaries just for this sort of work? Really, how rich some people were. Sarojbala bit her tongue as soon as the thought occurred to her. It was because they had hired her that she would actually be able to send her son some money, for there would be a bit left over after expenses.

She dreamt of money, but she was uneasy.

She had to go in and out of the tiger's cage every day.

Her daughter had instructed her not to talk too much. Just as much as was necessary in the course of work.

Of course, everyone here was busy. Badhi-Ma's son and daughter both went to office at nine in the morning, returning only at nine in the evening.

Saroj had come to know that the real work in this city was commuting. People worked and managed their households despite spending four or five hours every day on trains and buses and in cars—that was how they lived. But could this be called living? The people here were like sugarcane sticks pulped by the wheels of a juice-making machine. Raghu stayed in the flat through the day. Sarojbala came and went three or four times, doing all that Badhi-Ma needed. Raghu didn't like staying beyond seven-thirty, which was why Sarojbala was in charge of Badhi-Ma's dinner.

Sarojbala didn't sit down anywhere near Badhi-Ma, just in case an exchange led to a conversation. She bustled about, folding the old woman's clothes, reorganising the contents of her suitcases, placing fresh naphthalene balls in the clothing, lining the racks with newspaper.

The first few days had not been busy.

'What did you say your name is?'

'Saroj. Sarojbala.'

'What kind of name is Sarojbala? Are you sure it isn't Saryubala?'

'Hmm.'

'Saryubala? What's your mother's name? Where did you say your home is? Where did you live in Delhi? What does your son do?'

Badhi-Ma's daughter-in-law said she needed a photograph and proof of address. They had to be submitted to the police.

'You've never lived here, after all. Lucky your daughter's close by.'

'She's old, don't worry about her, Mausi. We've been here ten years, haven't we? Let Ma help Badhi-Ma for a few days, see how it goes, no need to pay if she doesn't do her job well.'

How bold this daughter of hers was! When her daughter told her that her mother was named Kaushalya and her father, Vishwanath, she had said, shaking with fear, 'I can't do this. I'll die of fright. What if you get into trouble? What if they find out?'

But this small, thin daughter of hers was not only courageous but also tough.

It was her spunk that allowed her to send her children to an English-medium school, engage private tutors for them, transforming herself and her family in speech, behaviour and habits. Sarojbala barely knew this woman.

'You have to do it,' her daughter had said angrily. 'You think I'm going to lose a three-thousand-rupee job because of your fear? Dozens of people will come running if they so much as snap their fingers—have you any idea?'

'But what if I say something wrong? What if something terrible happens to you?'

'Forget it, nothing will go wrong.' She tossed her head. 'Ten thousand human beings and four hundred cars are born in this city every day. There are ways to get papers for all of them. No one can do anything to you, take my word.'

Her daughter wasn't wrong. She had lived here for ten years and knew the place well. No one had the time to interfere in other people's affairs. No one had asked Sarojbala what she ate, what she put on her skin, how things were back home.

Because time hung heavy on Badhi-Ma's hands, she made Sarojbala sit down and chat sometimes, but she spoke about her own life rather than ask questions.

There was another characteristic this city had. A big heart. Humans, dogs, pigs, jackals—they were packed together, in congested chawls, in slums that resembled pigsties. But they looked after one another, gave way on the road, didn't stab each other in the back. Because everyone had to survive. Mumbai had realised that you cannot live unless you let live—and because it had, it stayed afloat on the Arabian Sea like a plate with a raised rim brimming with water.

Badhi-Ma went for a walk in the late afternoon in the clearing beneath the multistoreyed building. She was over eighty and did no chores at home—walking was her only form of exercise. She walked a measured five hundred steps in her room, with Sarojbala trailing behind. One of them walked for better digestion, and the other, to suppress hunger. It was amusing. Although Sarojbala was over sixty, she still had an erect frame. She did have a slight stoop, but her appetite was intact. She bathed her grandchildren, fed them, took them to school and brought them back—her daughter didn't have a moment to spare once she entered the Bakshis' home.

Badhi-Ma took her walk between five and six-thirty every evening. Saroj escorted her downstairs in the lift with care, strolling along with her. On her return, she gave the lady a glass of water and her medicines, followed by sweets, pudding or fruit juice. So many medicines for just one person! Sarojbala was astonished at the sight. Red, blue, yellow tablets, Ayurvedic pills, homeopathic globules, biochemical liquids—everything had an appointed hour. Sarojbala did not know how to tell the time, but no one here had found her out. Not that that proved to be a problem because Sarojbala could manage by the position of the sun, as she had all her life. And also, Badhi-Ma knew exactly when she had to be given each of her medicines, along with its dosage—she always called out loudly to Sarojbala to remind her.

Sarojbala had about an hour of free time before Raghu left. She used it to visit the park by the seaside, by herself or with her grandchildren. The waves crashed on the black boulders at high tide, seagulls cried, the wind blew furiously. And then, look at how far the water retreated at low tide, like a sulking schoolboy. A long stretch of the black boulders became visible, the air grew still, a terrible stench of stale fish spread everywhere, but still the sea was lovely. The sun set like a ball of fire in this sea every day. The moon rose, then sank in the water. Moonlight sent a column of light deep beneath the surface of the water, a magical pillar of gold, shimmering with the movement of the sea. Sometimes Sarojbala even had to spend the night with Badhi-Ma—the old woman was never to be left alone. Her son and daughter-in-law might have gone to the movies or a party, and they wouldn't be back before midnight. She spread out a mat near Badhi-Ma's feet and sat or lay down on it. That was when she observed this novel sport of the sea by night. The time she spent with the sea was entirely her own—during these moments she was nobody's mother, nobody's wife, nobody's mother-in-law. The sea at high tide swayed her heart, the gusts of wind unsettling her. The sea asked, what are you doing, Sarojbala, is this any way to live? Do you call this living? Concealing your own name, identity, attire, behaviour, everything? Your life is a lie. Sarojbala felt an upheaval within herself. To hell with all this, she told herself—I'll go back to Delhi, I'm sure I'll survive somehow. My daughter's lived here for ten years; she'll manage without me. Then, in bed at night, when she heard the rustling of the currency notes from her salary inside the pillowcase where she had stashed them, when she saw her grandchildren's freshly ironed white school uniforms hanging on the wall, she told herself, no, never mind, what use is the truth—let me spend some time with those who are struggling to escape the noose of poverty.

That was when she lay quietly, thinking of the long, golden archway in the night sea created by the moon. Sarojbala had never seen anything so beautiful in her life. There was no sea in Delhi—only a few sunbaked trees next to the tiny and dark shanty they lived in, besides dense undergrowth, large heaps of refuse and rows of shanties just like theirs. Closing her eyes, she slid down the golden pillar to the bottom of the ocean. From the light and waves, she tried to glean some comfort, some joy, for herself, even as her teardrops moistened her pillow at the recollection of the pitiful conditions her son and daughter-in-law lived in.

Early one morning Sarojbala woke up with a high fever, accompanied by a headache. It was morning, and yet her body wouldn't allow her to get out of bed—the thought bewildered her. Her daughter rushed back several times from the Bakshis' to check on her. Then, playing truant from her regular work, she went off to bathe Badhi-Ma.

Why didn't I give you a sheet at night? What was I thinking? Her daughter rushed off again, to manage the work at two households. Badhi-Ma's son and daughter-in-law had been to the airport last night. They had returned at two in the morning with their son. Saroj had been sitting on a mat near Badhi-Ma's feet; behind her was the open window through which the north wind blew. She hadn't dared sit on the other side, in case she didn't hear the bell ring. The sari draped across her back could not keep the wind at bay. She had been cold; it had seeped into her bones. Sarojbala had remembered that her warm clothes were in a bundle back in Delhi—two woollen sweaters and a thick shawl. She hadn't expected to stay on here till winter, which was why she hadn't brought them along. Now, as the chilly wind blew about her, she had tried to gain warmth by thinking about them. She did manage to wake up late at night to open the door and then go to her own room to sleep—after which she remembered nothing.

When she returned hesitantly to Badhi-Ma after two days of fever and splitting headaches, no one scolded her. There was a wave of happiness in the house. A handsome young man had come home from a foreign country. His name was Milind. Badhi-Ma's grandson. He had a thick head of hair, glasses, a fresh beard—holding his hand out to Saroj, he said, 'Hi!' Saroj was startled. He brought her a chair to sit on, making Badhi-Ma frown. Unwilling to annoy anyone, she fetched a mat instead and sat on it. Sarojbala was reminded of the golden archway in the water, made by the moon—it was moving about inside the house now.

Milind was always busy when at home, reading, working on the computer or repairing things. He didn't let Saroj touch the dishes he ate out of, doing them himself. Apparently, they had to cook for themselves over there and do the dishes too. There were no servants to do the household work in this land of rich people. Sarojbala was puzzled.

If there were no servants, if you had to do your work yourself, what was the difference between the rich and the poor? And what did the poor people do over there, for that matter?

How strange it was! Milind addressed her as Aunty and actually asked questions about her life. Saroj was no longer afraid. She stood behind Badhi-Ma when she ate, one hand on the old woman's chair in case she needed anything. Milind didn't insist on her sitting. He stood too, at the other end of the table. There were many things he wanted to know.

'What do you eat for dinner, Aunty? Rotis or rice?'

'Do you own land back home? What do you grow on it?'

'Which do you prefer—Bombay or Delhi?'

'Have you decided what you want your grandchildren to study when they grow up?'

At night, on her own mattress in her room, Sarojbala had a strange dream once or twice after Milind's arrival. It embarrassed her. She saw herself sitting in a soft velvet armchair, like the ones you saw at weddings, supplied by the people who provided all the furniture. In front of her was a steaming brew of tea, in a beautiful cup and saucer …

The dream was so wrong that Sarojbala hadn't even dared to tell her daughter.

Something had happened to her. When she went to the park on the way back from her grandchildren's school, or while she oiled Badhi-Ma's hair with warm coconut oil, only one image floated up in her mind. A thick head of hair, a tender beard. A fair, handsome, bespectacled face.

'Do you think I should shave my beard or let it grow, Aunty?' Milind wanted her opinion.

It was such a strange time. Sarojbala had never imagined that anything like this could happen. Milind went out on work sometimes, going out of town for two or three days. Sarojbala felt miserable. She lost her appetite, made mistakes at work, gave Badhi-Ma thirty drops of the medicine for the aching foot instead of twenty—as though her eyes were streaming with tears. And when Milind returned, she was filled with joy, as though flowers were blooming all over the house.

Her perceptive daughter did not miss her capricious behaviour. Smiling covertly, she said, 'These are foreign birds, they'll peck at the grains, but they won't enter the cage; they'll fly away. What will you do then?'

What would she do then? That was true. The thought haunted her even as she felt herself alive. What would she do? What could she possibly do? An unreal dream occupied her.

What if Milind took her away, far away, where people shook hands with the household staff and offered them chairs …

'You and your ridiculous ideas! Remember what your daughter said, don't they have labourers over there? Don't they make people work in factories? Who was it who brought black people as slaves from foreign lands?'

She didn't dare mention her dream to her daughter, as if that would shatter a fragile bowl of glass. Milind's day of departure really did arrive. He had been here a month and a half. How much longer could his holiday last? He had to study, finish his research.

He had shaved before leaving, his face looking softer and fairer now.

The flight was to leave at two in the morning. Milind would leave at ten-thirty, after dinner. Her daughter and son-in-law had dropped in to say goodbye. Her grandchildren had got fistfuls of chocolate. Now he was touching his parents' feet in respect. His grandmother was handing him a bowl of curd. If he wiped his hand on her sari afterwards, he would have a safe journey. Saroj gazed at him, her vision blurred, but she wasn't blinking. Milind came forward and hugged her. There was a packet on a chair for her.

'Here you are, Aunty, wear this when you feel cold.'

Milind draped a soft green shawl around her.

Instead of thinking of how comfortable she would be next winter, Sarojbala mourned—she felt as though the moon had splintered, sinking deep into the water along with the glittering pillar of gold. Stay safe, my son, wherever you are, may my lifetime be added to yours. And may God give you all the wealth in the world, may Allah give you all his blessings—with these words in her head, Shabnam Banu, mother of Bilkis Banu, wept, shedding from her soul the fear of living, dropping all the shame of her non-existence into the water of the Arabian Sea.

RULES OF THE GAME

This nap just before the evening is something of an addiction. Four days a week I go to work from eight to three. Glued to the desk. Taut with tension. Then back home to change out of work clothes and eat. The work stretches to twelve hours the other three days. There's no question of getting home before sunset. On these days, though, my eyes grow heavy with sleep after the meal. I sit on the sofa, turning over the pages of the unread newspaper, or leafing through a book. I try not to fall asleep, but eventually I give up and lay my head on the pillow. Heavy slumber like a fishing net filled with rocks draws me deep below the surface. The alarm goes off an hour later. I turn it down and go back to sleep. Not as deeply this time, but still, it clings to me like a fit of drunkenness. I feel as though I'm under a sheet of water glittering in the sunlight. Shami rouses me from sleep half an hour later. That is to say, he knocks on the door. I take another five minutes to get out of bed and splash some water on my face. The tray sits on the table, covered with lace or voile, with a teacup and teapot sitting on it. A couple of biscuits on a plate. Shami knows everything. There's no knock on the door today.

'Bihu! Bihu!' Shami is calling out. He's not supposed to, it irritates me. I spend less time than usual washing my face and go out. There's no tea on the table.

'Didn't you make any tea? Can't wake up properly without tea.'

'Something wrong with the wire.' Shami picks up the electric kettle to display its bottom. The plug at the end of the cable is burnt and blackened.

'How did this happen?'

Shami shrugs.

'Couldn't you smell it burning? Why didn't you make the tea on the gas stove?'

'Can't light it.'

'How strange, why not? Show me, try to light it.'

Standing beside him, I get a smell of sweat mixed with spices. The aroma of the kitchen sticks to Shami's body like a sticker. Maybe there's a similar scent beneath his skin. Uncombed hair above a singlet and shorts. His face only betrays the anxiety of being unable to light the stove.

'Oh no, you're holding the lighter the wrong way. What's the matter?'

There's no question of savouring the tea anymore.

I put the kettle to boil myself and make the tea.

Sitting on the sofa across from me, Shami says, 'I don't feel good, I can't remember a thing.'

'Oh? Can't remember? What do you mean?'

My world begins to shake.

'Do you need to see a doctor?'

'No, that's not it.' Shami shakes his head. 'Just some things.'

Since I go out every morning, Shami does all the housework. Getting Butaam ready for school and seeing him off into the bus, then fetching him home at two-thirty. Getting his clothes in order, giving him lunch. Butaam showers on alternate days. The water has to be checked for the right temperature. Butaam can manage the rest on his own.

What if Shami forgets to fetch Butaam one of these days?

'How can you say that? Have I ever?' Shami is angry, but he doesn't raise his voice.

It's true, he hasn't forgotten, but still …

…

A woman friend of Shami's arrives as evening falls. She lives in the flat on the right on the first floor of the same building as ours. Chilka was his classmate in college. Shami went on to get a master's degree, his friend didn't continue with her studies after her BA. She doesn't work, her husband is a used-car dealer. Chilu throws herself on our sofa, which catches my eye because she lowers herself gingerly when it comes to her own sofa. 'Shami is extremely stressed, Bihu,' she says. 'He can't cope.' I cannot understand which of Shami's tasks are stress-inducing. He's devoted to our son. Butaam, too, is happiest when with his father. When he doesn't have anything else to do, Shami gets pure joy out of ironing Butaam's clothes, I've seen this for myself.

Shami goes into his room as soon as Chilu arrives. I don't know that he likes her very much. Could he have called her over himself?

'How can you tell he's stressed?'

'He rang our doorbell today on his way back with Butaam. I thought he needed something. I opened the door to find

Butaam laughing away and Shami saying, sorry, it was a mistake.'

'Was it a very unnatural mistake?'

'The thing is that he's behaving differently these days. You haven't noticed, but he seems a little disheartened, absent-minded ...'

I could have said, 'If you've noticed, that's good enough.' Or something bitchier. I didn't. I've become canny these days. There's a month-long bank audit coming up, my days will stretch to twelve hours, Shami monitors the entire household, all I do is get some inputs from him and pay for things, sometimes order whatever we need online, but even that will be difficult now.

This is not the time to exasperate a neighbour like Chilka. And besides, Shami's on a downer, he's forgetting things. I have to think carefully about what I should do. Antidepressants will mean dozing all day, which will only add to my tension. Should I send him for counselling? Even getting an appointment takes ages, there are many more patients than counsellors. Men didn't go to them in such large numbers before. They had lives outside home, other male friends, drinking, sport, hookah bars. Even thirty years ago. Ever since the workplace rejected them and they turned into househusbands, they've been going through a strange devaluation. How many can have family businesses of their own? Opportunities for going out of the home have dropped, and the infamous masculine networking has all but vanished.

Women were already under pressure, both at home and outside of it. Having to labour like beasts of burden in domestic as well as work places had left them utterly harassed. Suddenly the government and industrial groups in the country seemed to discover simultaneously that women workers are much more productive. They don't go for frequent smoke breaks, they don't spend hours gossiping at others' workstations. The most they do outside of work is social media, but these platforms are deactivated in offices now. Working hours number between eight and twelve, without a break. But the workload back home has decreased. Some 60 to 80 per cent of corporate employees are women now, which has made the GDP go up in leaps and bounds. But men are half the sky, what if they are not happy?

Still, women are not under as much pressure at home. They dress smartly and are well-groomed. The homebound men assist the cooks and cleaners. They are the ones who look after the children, and either do a little work from home or engage themselves in the pursuit of knowledge. Police drones patrol the streets. Crime has dropped. Cabs to take women to and from work run on the roads round the clock. But there's a different problem also taking wing. Men are growing more depressed. Their sex drives are waning. Others must be suffering from the same memory losses as Shami.

Earlier, women had spent generations at home cooking and cleaning and bringing up children. No records of their depression have been documented. We have not heard of the caged life of women having an impact on their conjugal lives. Men can get by even when their female companions feel no desire. But if the husband is unwilling, there's nothing that the wife can do. So, assaults on women on the streets have dropped, while complaints of marital rape from men are increasing. This was unimaginable thirty years ago. I realise that patriarchy is just waiting with its head down for an opportunity to strike.

It will assert itself as soon as it gets the chance. How long it had taken for women to establish marital rape as just cause for divorce! The majority of judges are women now, but their sympathies are with men.

Shami's the one who heats up dinner every evening. I've been sticking to him this evening since he's been feeling low. Butaam can tell everything isn't all right between us. He's gone to his own room after dinner to watch an action film projected in a large size on the wall. He's seven, but having learnt words and maths at the age of three, he has an extremely active mind.

After dinner we dim the living room lights, switch on the concealed music system and sit down next to each other on the sofa the way we used to even a year or two after we were married. Shami was thirty-two then, a bright young man with dreams. He used to study ancient history, and was preparing for a PhD, gearing up to write papers. I'd advertised on a matrimonial site that I preferred a househusband. Shami was the most intelligent, straightforward and courteous among the twenty applicants. His only ambition was to visit archaeological sites in our country and around the world. It was all to my liking—the contract was drafted accordingly. Shami was going to look after the home. The child, too, once they were born. This was to be his contribution to the family and household. In return for money, which I would provide. We have spent ten years peacefully. We, or I?

Shami is immersed in the joy of bringing up Butaam. My workload keeps increasing, my responsibilities, my social standing. Shami writes papers from time to time and submits them to journals here and there. He's applied for a PhD but there hasn't been much progress. A PhD is the minimum qualification even to teach in a school. As a result, the PhD guides have their slots full. The coursework is online, but still, there's no time.

Suddenly it seems to me Shami has turned into an old man. No haircut, unkempt bristly beard flecked with white, a dirty T-shirt, his sharp appearance is a thing of the past. We haven't been out for dinner in a long time. I have work conferences even on weekends, parties with colleagues. I don't have to take him shopping, he can order things online himself. There used to be large malls earlier and people had grown addicted to going to shops and buying things. They have been demolished and turned into parks and gardens. All of them with semi-hemispherical roofs have clean air, purified, with extra oxygen. Butaam and Shami go to these places now and then. Shami pays great attention to bringing up our son, but what happened to our personal time?

'Let's go abroad, the Maldives have gone underwater but we can do Hawaii.' We'd been to the Midwest of the US with Butaam, but even that was four years ago. Many of the places on the coasts of various countries that were tourist hotspots have sunk beneath the sea now, and forest areas are all on fire. You have to look hard for places to visit.

Shami surprises me with his answer. 'I don't want to go anywhere. I've got a job offer. In the Emirates of Afghanistan. They're restoring their ancient monuments, and they want a team to document the whole thing. Seven others from India along with me.'

'When?'

'Early next month. Give me my passport, I won't need a visa.'

Afghanistan was in very bad shape in my mother's lifetime, but it's calm now. Women returned to work about ten years ago. The hijab is enough, they can go out without having to wear burqas. Even Afghanistan has realised the country can earn more if women go to work. Men in our country are in fact in a worse situation than Afghan women.

I am furious at what Shami has said. 'My bank audit is about to begin, Butaam's evaluation is coming up, I'll have to make fresh arrangements if you leave now, I'll have to hire a man full-time and train him. Do you understand? It'll take three months at least. Have you forgotten the terms of the contract? At least six months' notice. Want to see?'

Switching off the music, I attach the portable memory to my wristband. Where's the contract? Can't find it. I begin to sweat. All documents older than ten years have been erased. Watching the beads of perspiration on my brow, Shami says, 'How you've changed, Bihu! Do you think I can't go anywhere because I have no earnings? You are lost in your money and your important post at work. Can you stop me if I leave? I can ask for immediate separation, the marital rape law is on my side now. It won't even need any proof. What will you do?'

Shami and I sit side by side, looking at each other. I don't know this Shami. He has a smile on his face, but it's hurting me terribly. Shami will prove me guilty, obtain a separation and leave, and I will start my life afresh, balancing child-rearing and work. I will regress exactly as much as I had progressed. Even more important, I will be held responsible, without evidence, for a crime I have never committed. I've never forced Shami, have I? I lay my head on my arm and weep.

Shami has turned the music on again. The room is filled with an evening glow. He's sitting next to me, touching my hair again like the old days. 'I'm not going anywhere, Bihu,' he's saying, 'but come back to yourself. Whenever I look at you, I feel I'm seeing an empty cage from which the bird has flown away. If you come back, I won't have to go anywhere. Where do you think I can go looking for historical monuments leaving Butaam and this house behind?'

I stop weeping and tell myself, as if it's so easy to come back. I've gone so far away into the blue of the sky. That blue there means breaking my shackles. Forever. Once you've learnt to fly, not even love can draw you back. For thousands of years, I have played the game of home-housewife-family with great love, but freedom is still far away.

I email Shami his passport, which is stored in my wristband, wipe my eyes and sit up. Let me free him. He's a man, he wasn't born to be chained. Let him still be Butaam's, still be mine. I'll rebuild the rules of the old game, the ones I'd assumed had been wiped out.

ADDRESS OF OBLIVION

Bakul stopped abruptly on the stairs on her way to the first floor. A tote bag hung from her shoulder, and she had another bag with clothes in her hand. Shiben thought they were too heavy for her. 'Give the bags to me, Boudi,' he said from the back, 'you go on ahead.' Still Bakul wouldn't move. The stairs were covered by a swarm of bees, from the bottom to the top. Had a beehive been broken somewhere? Bakul retreated fearfully. Atish had made arrangements to drink tea in the open. She heard the sound of loud laughter. No one had broken a hive. A strong gust of wind in the afternoon had dislodged it. They really should have broken it earlier, though. It was huge. There, on the second-floor parapet.

Bakul didn't dare look up. What if they stung her on the face? Shiben noticed the portion that had broken off. It was lying beside the draw-well. Crystals of golden honey in its cells. A multitude of bees buzzing over it.

'You've become so urban, Bakul.'

Did Atish address her by her name or as Boudi earlier? Bakul couldn't recollect.

Meanwhile Shiben spoke up. 'Keep going, Boudi, walk normally, as though they aren't there. Bees sting only if you disturb them, not otherwise.' Passing through the net of countless bees flying all around her, Bakul went into the long room on the first floor to find four single beds laid out next to one another. White sheets, blankets folded near their feet. Clean pillowcases. Here too there were clumps of bees on the ceiling, in the corners of the walls. The sight sent shivers down her spine. 'The bathroom's outside, though, Boudi. You'll get a bucket and water. Come, we'll get some tea.' The bees displayed no reaction to her entrance, remaining suspended or flying about as before. Bakul was somewhat reassured at this. Had they realised then that Bakul had nothing to do with their hive being broken?

An attempt had been made to create a garden in the open expanse outside. Small flowering plants in red soil, along with seeds of canna lily and geranium. Shiben poured the tea from a teapot, Shyamal gave her some pakoras. Atish was like a permanent boss, without any specific responsibility besides supervision. 'So much food now? There's dinner too …' Bakul hesitated. Shiben said, 'Dinner's a long way away, Boudi. Who knows when Shyamal here will enter the kitchen—at least five hours after that—' Taking a chilli pakora, Shyamal said, 'We've been waiting for you since lunchtime. I could have fetched you on my bike if you'd taken the Lodhashuli road. Didn't know you were coming via Gopiballabhpur.' There were plenty of options, she could have taken the train to Kharagpur too. No matter what the route, Shyamal would have picked her up. 'I've been thinking of you ever since the foundation stone was laid, Bakul. Even more than you, of Ashim.' Everyone had dreamt of a place like this. Almost all of life had passed in fulfilling the dream.

An asphalt road ran outside the farmhouse. The river ran on the other side. The late afternoon breeze signalled the presence of the Subarnarekha. Did water have a smell of its own? A sal forest had descended all the way to the edge of the water. An enthusiastic Shiben had taken Bakul to the riverbank already. Since it was the middle of February, it wasn't exactly overflowing. The trail they took down the slope, stepping on stones and staying clear of the cracks in the ground, was littered with thermocol plates and glasses and cola bottles left behind by picnickers. 'So dirty,' Bakul had said, steering herself away from them. 'Look how they leave the garbage behind. Can't there be a drum or something?' 'We'll take care of everything slowly, Boudi, we've only just begun. Tourists have begun coming again after corona, even if only three or four a month. Look at the river, how can you have eyes only for the rubbish?'

The river wasn't very wide here. But looking upstream revealed it flowing towards them with a body of bluish-green water, like destiny. Bakul sat down on a rock, as though protecting herself from the litter around her. Was she turning into someone who made a fetish out of cleanliness? The river was free of thought. After all, it absorbed all the blows and torture people inflicted on it to keep its canvas of water open to view. For that one person out of a million who yearns for something beautiful. Had Bakul's own longing for beauty evaporated somewhere within her? And then the conspiracy of the bees on the way upstairs. Something between assault and disdain. She had drunk her tea, and now she filled her breast with the air in which the smells of the water and the sal forest had mingled. The late afternoon light in the sky had made way for the deep pink of twilight. The stars had started coming to life in ones and twos. The moon was nearly full, its beams sliding down to the house. The tall trees bathed in the water of the moonlight. Such beauty was far from rare for those who had invited her here. Atish lived in Jhargram. He had already retired from his schoolteacher's job. Shyamal had a small business in Lodhashuli, doing up wedding venues. Shiben was a cultivator, not too far away. His daughter had just passed her final medical college examination. Khaga Mahato would be here later at night. He lived two villages away. There was a jatra performance, so he would come afterwards—he too wanted to meet Bakul Boudi.

Bakul's life was a wide-open empty space. A reverberating wail ran through it like a 1960s Bengali song. The loan on the four-hundred-square-foot flat had been paid back seven years ago. She took the train to school from home, and then from school to home, getting back into the box. These days she often had a headache in the evening. She didn't even feel like warming the food after taking it out of the fridge, simply eating the cold vegetables with some muri and going to bed. The next day she threw away the stale rice. The occasional school picnic. The teachers threw parties sometimes. That was about all. Now and then men had been attracted to the working childless widow, expressing their desire for marriage. When she rejected their proposals, they spread slander about her. Widow? What! Bakul was considering herself a widow, how strange. Ashim was not dead, he was missing. He had disappeared. Or had he been abducted? Killed? Someone whose body hadn't been recovered or about whose being alive no news had been received even after thirty years was dead, wasn't he?

Someone had made her tea after a long time, fried pakoras for her. They would probably serve her dinner too. The aroma of cooking wafted out from the half-covered terrace of the building. 'Country chicken?' 'Absolutely. We don't do broilers here. Cabbage with fish heads. Catla kalia. You do eat catla?' Bakul smiled quietly. What she liked eating, and what she didn't, were things that no longer mattered to her. So long as there was something to eat. Bakul didn't enjoy cooking. It was difficult to cook just for herself, she was too lazy for it. But she didn't need anyone else to dress well, just herself and the mirror. Bakul still liked saris of fine fabric. Flowers in her hair. A visit to the beauty parlour once every two months. She didn't look like she was on the other side of fifty.

Bakul's neck was aching from gazing at the sky, but even then she couldn't lower her head. The constellations were in full view now. That was Orion over there. Cassiopeia far to the north. Sirius kept waiting in anticipation, but it seemed as though the head of Orion couldn't be found. These stars so far in the distance were clear, but the man close to her had turned into a blur.

During dinner Shiben talked about how it was Atish who had put the land and the house together. It was a small plot of land at first, then he had added more. The draw-well. A submersible pump. The garden. One step at a time. Shiben, Shyamal and Khaga were of limited means. They only supplied vegetables and sheets and blankets, whatever they could afford. Shyamal had got the beds made by the carpenter in his company. Separating the bones from the fish head, Bakul had asked a simple question out of curiosity: 'Do you get enough tourists to cover costs?' From the adjoining table Atish had answered solemnly, 'We didn't build this to make money. There are no calculations of profit and loss. When there are visitors we let them stay here, we make some arrangements for them, that's about it. They pay some money, the building is used. This is an address. For oblivion. When there's nothing left in life, nothing or no one to depend on, no hope, people can come here. To go into oblivion.' Bakul laughed. 'I have no one to depend on, Atish, but I have hope. I don't want to go into oblivion.' Atish kept eating without a response, his face lowered. It was clear Bakul's comment had affected him. She refused more chicken despite Shiben imploring her to take a second helping. No sweets either. Khaga had probably had a few drinks at the jatra performance. But he had brought plantain leaves from his garden. He served the food to the accompaniment of singing and dancing.

The stairs to the upper floors had no railing. The darkness had subdued the light all the way down. Shiben guided Bakul with the flashlight from his mobile phone. 'Atish has changed, he's obsessed with this building, Boudi. The things he says give me goose pimples. He says, won't need anyone else, I'll take this dear friend of mine whom life has given such a hard deal down to the river. We'll be chatting. He won't even realise how close to the water he is. When he's at the edge all it'll take is a slight shove from the back. No one will find out. Anyone calling him will be told his phone is switched off, they will keep getting the same message, the sun will get stronger, he will be gone far, far away ...'

In the long room the disoriented bees were still flying about. They had gone mad with grief for the home that no longer existed after being smashed to pieces. Bakul was a little fearful about going in. She saw the bees that were sticking to the wall earlier plummeting to the floor now, dead. Their hive was their entire life, they flew around frenziedly only in fear of having to live without a home, and when they couldn't fly, they died. Bakul had had no home since Ashim had left. But she was still alive, alone. Clinging to a wall. Ashim would come back one day. Like his fellow warriors, a little stooped, aged, balding in front, with sunken cheeks and eyes like those of dead fish, devoid of dreams. So be it but let him return. Bakul wouldn't take long to weave dreams again.

She was visiting the area after twenty years, having arrived late in the afternoon two days ago. On the first few occasions she had come here to enquire about Ashim, the district of Midnapore had not yet been bifurcated. Just in case he had returned. After all, his aged parents lived in their home in the village, an uncle too. Gopiballabhpur here was the centre of the protest movement over sharing the harvest. In the 1960s and early '70s peasant leaders had occupied the land to establish their rights to a fair share of the crops. They had avenged the tyranny of the moneylenders by taking over the farmland. Their comrades in the revolt against the Brahmin landowners included students and the educated youth. Many of those who had joined them were dead; the survivors were old, hermits in their homes. Ashim's uncle was one of them.

Bakul's family used to live in the same neighbourhood, which was protected from prying eyes by a tall wall. The houses stood next to one another. Most of them were in ruins now. Only one of the walls and the front door of the house Bakul had lived in remained now. There was a dense bamboo thicket within the neighbourhood, where various kinds of birds flew about. The cuckoos had begun calling even before March. After the movement the party split into two, the Left came to power, but the fires in Jangal Mahal didn't go out fully. Pro-government leftist leaders faced police action even in the 1990s. Shyamal had spent two years in hiding in north Bengal. Shiben had gone underground right here. Khaga Mahato feared no one. Let them kill me, he declared, and continued to live in the village on his own terms. Buying peace didn't prove any easier just because their own people were in the government. The one who managed to avoid police action was Atish—he didn't have to escape. The only one to disappear was Ashim. Bakul was in Calcutta then, having started a new job at a school. Some people had abducted him near the river at the edge of the village. Who were these people? Bakul returned to the village in tears on being informed about Ashim. Later Atish stayed at Bakul's house when visiting Calcutta. Several times. Bakul hadn't fulfilled his desire. She had come to these parts repeatedly to look for Ashim, although the search was becoming meaningless with the passing of time. Still, she had maintained her resolve to keep making the visits by bus or train for five or six years. Then the scene began to blur.

The cold made the hair on Bakul's arms stand on end as she went into the room from the tiny bathroom outside. The moon was much higher, radiating its beams and an iciness too. She was visiting Ashim's uncle after a long time, much too late. Paralysis had slurred his speech. He had been asking to see Bakul. His wife had rung her. 'Come by, he wants to see you. Who knows when he might leave us.' Bakul couldn't understand what he was saying. His wife placed her ear close to his lips to explain to Bakul.

Walking into the distance along the riverbank at dawn, Bakul could tell the cold was actually rising from within herself. Even if it was warmer during the day, the mornings were cool. The river seemed dispassionate, detached. This village stood at the border of three states. Did rivers realise how political borders were created, how people went to war over their waters, wars that never stopped? Bakul hadn't slept very well at night. The men had slept on rows of beds in the large hall downstairs. The sounds of their chattering and laughter. The joy of everyone gathering in the same place after ages. Ashim could have been among them. But no, why should he have been with them? He would have gone to bed upstairs beside Bakul. She kept waking up and checking the time on her phone. The windows were closed for fear of the bees. And yet, she felt Atish was standing outside.

...

Shiben and Shyamal had begun preparing breakfast for Bakul. After such a heavy dinner she could easily have skipped the morning meal. But who was to explain this to them? She would have to take the bus back after breakfast. She was alone with herself now, longing to go into the river. To feel the touch of water on her feet. Her childhood swims in the river would not come back by jumping into the Subarnarekha now. Just as Ashim wouldn't, either.

Going very close to the water, Bakul could tell even without looking over her shoulder that Atish was standing behind her. Did he know Bakul would go down to the river at dawn?

Atish, Ashim's uncle had said. Atish knows who took Ashim away. His wife had taken her ear close to his lips and then told her. Do you know where Ashim is, Atish?

Bakul turned around from where she stood at the edge of the water and fixed a serene pair of eyes on Atish.

AN ASHOKA CENTRE FOR TRANSLATION SERIES

This new translation series introduces English-language readers to some of the best Indian works of fiction, both modern and classic, that have sustained a wide readership in their source languages. Selected by the respective translators and co-published with Westland Books, the titles in this series are being presented by the Ashoka Centre for Translation as part of its commitment to foster India's multilingual ethos.

To find out more about the Ashoka Centre for Translation's initiatives, please log on to translation.ashoka.edu.in.

This translation of Anita Agnihotri's stories has been supported by Rahul Mookerjee in loving memory of Subimal Mookerjee, a Bengali who—from Presidency College, Calcutta, to the Royal Naval College, Dartmouth, and back to the shores of India—thought in English.